Chambers of the Heart

Chambers of the Heart

LaShayla Teemer Dyer

www.astapublications.com

First Printing, Asta Publications, LLC, trade paperback first edition January 2015

ISBN 13: 978-1-934947-80-7

Manufactured in the United States of America

Dedication

I dedicate this book to my grandmother, Mrs. Leola Chambers (October 12, 1922-November 3, 2004) whose words, touch, and food could soothe my soul. I wish you were here to see the things that God has done and to celebrate with me. You are forever in my heart.

Acknowledgements

My **God** is awesome. I asked and **He** said, "Yes."

To my husband, **Kendrick Dyer**, you are the love of my life. Thank you for loving me unconditionally, for not allowing me to limit myself, for supporting me, and for understanding my passion for creative writing. Thank you for being my number one fan!

To my loving, intelligent, and creative son **Tylin**, you inspire me to be a better person. I am so proud of YOU!

To my loving, intelligent, and charismatic son **Tyndil**, you inspire me to be a better person. I am so proud of YOU!

To my parents, **Nathaniel** and **Leola C. Teemer**: Thank you for teaching me about God, His love, His Word, and His wonders. Thank you for teaching me about love, the value of family, and the power of prayer. **Mommy**, thank you for sharing your *Pearls of Wisdom*, for pouring into my life, and for requiring me to stir up the gifts within me. Thank you for teaching me to open my heart to others, to love all people the same, and to be a blessing to others.

To my sister, **Natalie Teemer Washington, Esq.**, thank you for your powerful words, honest heart, persistent spirit, and legal eyes. To my brother-in-law, **Captain David Washington** of the US Army, thank you for serving our country and for supporting me.

To my sister, **Nayonda Teemer Gibson**, thank you for your honesty, your encouragement, and your wisdom. To my brother-in-law, **Maurice Gibson**, thank you for supporting me in all that I do.

To my sister and my brother-in-law, **LaShonda** and **Bernard Tyler**, thank you for inspiring me.

To my sister, **Chequita Phillips,** thank you for inspiring me.

To my **Chambers Family,** thank you for always being a loving and supportive family. Thank you for your prayers.

To my friends, **Shawntay Coleman** and **Kelena King**, thank you for your many years of friendship.
> *"A friend loveth at all times."* Proverbs 17:17

To **Professor William Derrick Harris,** thank you for your editing services and encouraging me to share Jade and Donovan's story with the literary world.

To **Assuanta, Rachel, Amanda**, and all of the **staff** at **Asta Publications, LLC**, thank you for your support and guidance, and for making my dream a reality!

"For where your treasure is, there your heart will be also."
Matthew 6:21

Prologue

Jade stood up behind her mahogany desk and looked around her office. Although she'd decorated over seven years ago, the decorations were still tasteful. She and her husband Jonothan had shared the office space, as they had done most things since they were married. Together they created a haven where they could work that was still warm and inviting to others. They painted the room themselves. The office walls were a shade of green called Sweet Annie and the trim and chair railing were painted café au lait.

Jade walked over to touch the small space beside the door. She ran her hand gently along the wall. Sliding down to sit on the floor, she closed her eyes and remembered the day she and Jonothan painted the office.

"Jade, I thought we agreed that I'd paint the small spaces." Jonothan said, as he kissed her neck after walking behind her.

"Yeah, well this one wasn't as small as the others. I thought that I could paint it without making a mess." Jade turned to face him. She kissed him softly on the lips before whispering, "But I guess I was wrong. Honey, I was really trying to help."

Truth be told, Jade was a horrible painter. Jonothan would have been done painting hours ago, if she hadn't been "helping" him.

Jonothan looked at the green paint splattered on the trim of the door frame. "Uh huh, you did good," he said, taking a moment to nibble on her neck. "I'll get the paint and we can touch up the door trim." He winked and walked across the room to retrieve the paint.

"Sorry," Jade said in a singsong voice.

"I'm not. I enjoyed you today." Walking back to her, he leaned down to kiss her softly. "Now let's get started on this trim." Jonothan stood behind Jade and pressed his body into hers and said, "I love you."

"I love you," Jade moaned. "Jonothan, we need to finish…

then maybe…we can…"

"Alright, it's just hard to stay focused with you around. Especially, in those shorts."

Jonothan guided Jade's hand up and down. Together they repainted the door frame.

"We did it and it's perfect," Jade said.

"Everything's perfect with you, Mrs. Jonothan McNeir."

Jade opened her eyes. Jonothan was the one who had made her life, her world, perfect. She shifted her eyes to the space where Jonothan's desk once sat. She'd replaced it with a loveseat and chair for decorative purposes. On the wall directly behind the loveseat was a beautifully framed limited edition painting of *Morals of Life* by Aaron Reed. It had been Jonothan's favorite work of art. Her eyes shifted to her workspace, where her favorite paintings hung over her desk: *Beauty of Color* and *Expressions of Joy* by Tim Ashkar.

The furniture was mahogany and very traditional. Floor-to-ceiling bookshelves covered one wall. The design was Jonothan's idea, as the bookshelves slid apart to reveal financial and other important business files. The bookshelves were tastefully decorated with silk ivy, books, Mahogany Princess figurines, and picture frames. Jade walked over to the bookshelves and placed her hands on the first Mahogany Princess figurine that Jonothan had given her. It was called *"In Love."*

Jade picked up the figure and carried it with her as she sat on the loveseat. Jonothan motivated Jade to live outside of the constraints that she had set for herself. She believed that she could do anything when she was with him. "Come on, Jade, we never know what tomorrow holds, so let's try it !"

Since their marriage, Jade skied, rode horses, rode motorcycles (owned a hot pink Ducati), sky dived, zip lined, rock climbed, and now painted like a professional. She'd tried things that would have never been on her bucket list. Jade still couldn't believe that Jonothan had gotten her to zip-line twice during their trip to Jamaica.

She glanced around the office again, and Jonothan was everywhere. His spirit consumed the area. He was everywhere, but then he wasn't...she couldn't touch him, and he couldn't hold her. He was gone. Her mind could not compartmentalize the memories and her heart could not let go.

Yes, the office was still charming, but it was no longer a haven. Jade took a deep breath and moved to the large window that offered her a generous view of Summer, GA. She rubbed her arms as a chill coursed through her body. Although the weather was cold, with temperatures in the low 40's, Jade's chill had nothing to do with the weather. She attempted to hold in her tears, but could not. She was drowning in feelings of melancholy. She moved to view her image in the full-length mirror that adorned one of the walls in the office.

Jade didn't recognize herself. Her reflection was the epitome of grief. Her hair was pulled back in a tight bun and she had lost more than sixty pounds, causing her family and friends to worry about her physical and emotional well-being. Grief had consumed her mind, her heart, and her life. How could her family and friends not understand her sense of loss? Love and life had been taken from her, again. Jade's reality was that only her body had survived, for she had buried her heart along with her husband Jonothan and their unborn daughter, whom they'd planned to name Amber.

Jade was flooded with emotions and she looked down at her bridal set. Then she clutched her necklace, a 14-karat rose gold necklace with three charms, a Briolette Diamond Angel charm, a baby booty charm with an amber-colored stone, and a disc pendant with "Amber" engraved on it. Jonothan had given her the necklace with the Diamond Angel charm on their wedding day. The gift was affirmation of his unconditional love for her. The amber charm and disc pendant were also gifts from Jonothan, but one that he had not had the opportunity to give her. Jade found the gifts and a card hidden in Jonothan's nightstand drawer after his death.

Although it had been three years since Jonothan and

Amber's deaths, it seemed like yesterday. The grief, despair, pain, and loneliness were overwhelming for her. She closed her eyes, took a deep breath, and counted backwards from fifty. When Jade reached zero, she returned to her desk and continued to review the rezoning proposal to the city for an expansion to Holly Health and Community Service Center. The expansion to Holly Health symbolized a memorial for Jonothan.

Jonothan, Jade, and their friend Emanuel founded Holly Health and Community Service Center ten years ago. The center provided medical care, mental health counseling, and enrichment programs to low-income families in Summer, Georgia. Jonothan had been the Medical Director and physician, Emanuel a licensed clinical social worker, was the Director of Clinical Services, and Jade was the Executive Director. After Jonothan's death, Jade and Emanuel hired a new physician, Dr. Teresa Stallion.

Now three years later, Holly Health continued to grow, meeting the needs of the community it was founded to serve. Teresa had inquired about becoming an equal partner. Although Jade trusted Teresa and knew that she was dedicated to Holly Health, it was difficult for Jade to consider Teresa taking Jonothan's place in the business.

Jade reached up to undo her bun when her cell phone rang. It was her best friend, Tia.

"Hey, what are you doing?" Tia asked.

"I'm standing in front of the mirror in my office looking at this awful bun! You should have told me that it looks awful--that I look awful. How could you let me look like this for so long?"

"Hello, is this Jade?" Tia responded sarcastically. "The bun is horrible, but not as horrible as those dark clothes you're wearing."

"Tia, I think I am going to take some time off. I need to… you know," Jade said.

"Are you okay? Do you want me to come? Hold on."

Jade took a deep breath, not sure of what to do next.

Tia decided to include Onyx, Jade's sister on the call. The trio were best friends.

"Onyx, are you there?"

"Yeah, I am. What's going on? Make it quick; I'm at work," Onyx responded.

Tia spoke first. "Jade's thinking about taking some time off."

"Jade, what's going on?" Onyx asked.

"I'm tired. I feel like I am drowning and that life is passing me by," Jade said.

"Jade, is there anything that we can do?" Tia asked.

"No, I just need to get away."

"How much time are you going to take off?" Onyx asked.

"I don't know," Jade responded.

"I think that it's a great idea... We've been badgering you for three years to return to the land of the living," Onyx said.

Tia laughed, "Oh, thank God! I know the perfect place for you to go: my vacation home on St. Simons Island."

"Tia, I can't impose on you," Jade insisted.

"Oh, Girl, please. The house is just sitting there and I don't have time to enjoy it. Besides, you need this time; it's been three years. You'll love St. Simons Island, it's beautiful and serene. Stay as long as you need."

"Come on, Jade. Meet me there on Saturday, check things out. If you like it, I'll help you settle in and acquaint yourself with St. Simons and the city of Brunswick. Cheryl, Monique, and Emanuel can handle things while you're away. Besides, I need you to decorate the house, make it charming and calming. We'll go over a budget for you to decorate and make arrangements for any repairs. Decorating the house would be therapeutic, right? Jade?" Tia persisted.

Jade laughed. "Therapeutic or just free labor?"

"Jade, you should go," Onyx said. "Go let your hair down, wear a bikini, and do something to that house. We both know Tia hasn't done a thing to it.

"Hey! I'm on the phone. I can hear you," Tia yelled to Onyx. They all laughed.

Jade took another deep breath and asked, "Tia, are you sure?"

"Yes. The house is yours for as long as you like. Listen. I have to make a call. So I'll talk to you both later tonight," Tia answered.

"Love ya!" Jade said.

"Me, too," Onyx replied.

"Me, three," Tia said.

"Bye!" they said in unison as they disconnected.

A faint smile crossed Jade's face. She had decorated Tia's other homes over the years. They shared similar taste in furniture styles, art work, and color palettes. Jade enjoyed decorating and Tia despised it. Going to St. Simons could be therapeutic indeed.

Jade removed the hair pins from the bun and her hair fell over her shoulders. She picked up the phone and called Monique, her Executive Assistant and Mentee.

"Monique, please let Emanuel and Teresa know that I need to see the three of you in my office in ten minutes."

When they arrived to Jade's office, everyone was speechless at the sight of Jade with her hair down. They were even more shocked when Jade informed them that she was taking six months off.

*****

"Is Jade really thinking of taking some time off?" Tia thought back to her conversation with Jade. "I don't know what happened, but thank you God!" Tia smiled, full of hope that Jade was on a path towards healing. The chiming sound from her computer prompted Tia's thoughts to return to her work. She needed to call a parent to schedule an Individualized Educational Plan meeting.

"Good afternoon, this is Ms. McNeir. May I speak to Mr. Johnson? I am calling about his daughter Kamia."

"Ms. McNeir, I will put the call through to Mr. Johnson. If you experience difficulty with the connection, please call me back."

"Ms. McNeir, is everything okay with my daughter?"

"Yes, Mr. Johnson. Kamia is fine. I'm her new Speech and Language Pathologist. We need to schedule a meeting to update Kamia's Individualized Education Plan. During the meeting we will discuss Kamia's progress and update her speech and language goals for the remainder of the school year. Are you available to meet with the IEP Team on December 6th at 3:15 p.m.? I sent a letter home today, but I felt compelled to call you personally. Kamia is an extraordinary child. I don't want her challenge with articulation to hinder her confidence."

"Ms. McNeir, my baby is an extraordinary child. Ms. Evelyn, the girls' nanny, and I will attend the meeting. I look forward to meeting you."

Tia thought that there was something familiar about Mr. Johnson's voice. She looked at his name and contact information and thought that it couldn't be who she thought it was. Tia looked forward to their meeting, too.

*****

Four Days Later

Donovan was thirty minutes late for Kamia's IEP Meeting. He called to notify Ms. Evelyn that he would be late and she ensured him that she would arrive to the meeting at the scheduled time. Donovan called the school and left a message for Ms. McNeir. Donovan was a single father, but his daughters were his world. He attended all school meetings, events, and extracurricular activities when he was in town. His girls were his number one priority and he wanted them to always know that.

He arrived at the school at 4 p.m. and the school secretary informed him that everyone was waiting for him in the classroom.

When Donovan entered the classroom he was pleasantly surprised to find Ms. Evelyn and the IEP team eating and laughing. In the center of the table was a platter of chicken salad with crackers, a fruit platter, a lemon pound cake, and bottled waters. Ms. Evelyn had clearly charmed Ms. McNeir and the IEP team with food, and probably tales of the girl's mischievousness.

Donovan glanced around and greeted everyone, "Good afternoon everyone, please accept my apology for being late."

Tia McNeir was initially startled by the masculine voice until she looked into the eyes of his familiar face. Tia smiled, *it was him. It was really him.*

Tia stood to extend her hand to Donovan, "Mr. Donovan, I'm Ms. McNeir."

"Good afternoon, Ms. McNeir. It's a pleasure to meet you."

"Good afternoon, the pleasure is mine." Tia greeted Donovan with a hand shake and a head nod. Donovan's smile was silent confirmation that he understood the need for professional camaraderie between them. Tia was new to Tyler Academy's private school system and was unsure of the political climate.

Once Donovan was seated, the meeting began and proceeded quickly. Donovan was pleased with Kamia's progress from the previous year and accepted the IEP goal recommendations for the new school term. The meeting was adjourned. The IEP team thanked Ms. Evelyn for the food and beverage that she brought in for the meeting.

Tia extended her hand and said, "Mr. Johnson and Ms. Evelyn, again it was a pleasure to meet both of you."

Donovan gave Tia his business card. On the back he'd written, "Let's meet for dinner, lunch, or coffee to catch up, D."

Tia was ecstatic. She couldn't believe that it was Donovan. She hadn't seen him since college. She couldn't wait to call Onyx.

*****

"Onyx, can you talk?"

"Yes, but make it quick. I'm on my way to a meeting."

"Onyx, I saw Donovan today."

"Donovan, who?" Onyx asked, annoyed.

"Donovan Johnson."

"Really! Where? Is he married or dating anyone?" Onyx asked.

Tia filled Onyx in on her encounter with Donovan. "Can you believe that?" Tia sighed, "Onyx, maybe we should..."

"Yes, I'm thinking the same thing. Listen I'll call you later." Onyx said, ending the call.

Tia thanked God for His timing and His divine intervention.

Chapter One

J ade sat looking out at the glistening, beautiful Atlantic Ocean. She inhaled deeply. The refreshing, warm sea air and the sound of the waves soothed her senses. Already the awakening sun was peeking through the clouds. It was a beautiful May day--a hot one, but beautiful nonetheless. She loved spending time here in the early morning. It was her quiet time to reflect and give thanks. Most of the residents in the beach community were still sleeping.

Jade smiled, thinking of her friendships with Onyx and Tia. Onyx was not just her sister, she was her best friend, too. They were sixteen months apart and had always been extremely close. Jade wasn't sure how she would survive college without Onyx, until she met Tia. They met the first day of college orientation, anxious and annoyed with the uncertainty of their lives. They instantly became soul sisters. Her mom always said, "Real girlfriends should be few in number, but you should trust them like a sister…God made sisters for sharing laughter and wiping tears." She trusted Onyx and Tia with all her secrets and they had certainly shared a world of laughter and rivers of tears. If it hadn't been for Onyx and Tia, she wouldn't have survived the darkest times of her life.

Jade was so proud of her sister. Onyx had a phenomenal career as a pilot in the United States Army. Her professional love was aviation and her personal love was the Black Hawk helicopter. Onyx was promoted to Lieutenant Colonel last year. Jade, Ms. Pearl, and Tia flew to Hawaii for the ceremony. Jade giggled, thinking about her mother's decision to stay in Hawaii.

"Jade, I think that I need to stay here with Onyx. She has made the Army, her unit, and that helicopter her life. I feel in my spirit that something is wrong. "

Onyx initially asked Jade to speak to their mother, but both knew that the effort would be useless. Her mother, Pearl, was a strong, intelligent woman with a gift of discernment. There was no one or nothing that would change her mother's mind. Jade's mind wandered back to Tia. Where had the time gone? They had been friends for over fifteen years. Tia was a successful, adventurous, and free-spirited person. She was a speech and language pathologist who contracted with public and private school systems throughout the United States to implement the federal grant funded program, *More than Words* to improve verbal and non-verbal communication skills of elementary school children.

Tia and Onyx were both a perfect example of the meaning of the verse from Proverbs 17, "A friend loveth at all times."

Jade would be eternally grateful for Tia and Onyx. They both had insisted Jade come to this magnificent oasis. St. Simons was a beautiful and peaceful island. The lighthouse, St. Simons Island Light, located on the southern tip of the island, was an added delight.

The sound of the bell from the lighthouse pulled Jade from her thoughts. She had been sitting on the beach writing prayers in her journal. Her mother told her as a child that God heard all prayers, even those never spoken. She hoped that He would accept her written prayers, for she couldn't find the strength to speak. Her father taught her that God concerned Himself with the same things that concerned her. Even in her darkest times, her faith had not wavered; she just didn't exercise it. The last entry was a poem and a prayer Jade had written down twice, once in her journal and once on a loose piece of paper. The poem, entitled "Trust", was by an unknown Author:

We trust that beyond absence there is a presence.
That beyond the pain there can be healing.
That beyond the brokenness there can be wholeness.
That beyond anger there may be peace.

That beyond hurting there may be forgiveness.
That beyond the silence there may be the word.
That beyond the word there may be understanding.
That through understanding there is love.

The prayer reminded her of the scripture, "*For I know the plans I have for you, declares the LORD, plans to prosper you and not to harm you, plans to give you hope and a future.*" *Jeremiah 29:11*

Jade released the poem and prayer written on the loose paper into the water, and turned around, sensing that she was being watched. She didn't see anyone. A gentle breeze brushed her face, and she heard a whisper so soft and angelic that it willed her heart to accept its message: "There is no hurt on earth that Heaven cannot heal."

Jade inhaled another deep, fortifying breath. She attempted to hold in her tears, but lost the battle. As she turned to leave the beach, she saw a silhouette of a man on the horizon. She whispered, "Lord, thank you for my angel."

*****

Donovan sat on the beach and listened to the waves as they came ashore. He'd told Ms. Evelyn and the girls that they were taking a "summer trip" to St. Simons Island. The truth was Donovan had followed his lost love to this island on a whim and a prayer.

He had been watching Jade from afar for about an hour. He wiped a lone tear from his left eye. Mutual friends told him that she was still grieving her loss. But he wasn't aware of the toll that grief was having on her, and it broke his heart. She had lost a considerable amount of weight and seemed so small and fragile. His first instinct was to pull her into his arms and protect her, but he knew that she would not be receptive to him. He had to pray for guidance on how he should handle the situation.

Donovan's mind went back to the first day he laid eyes on

Jade at JC Chambers State University, during their sophomore year. Jade was wearing a lavender and sage-colored sundress, and she automatically stood out on the crowded campus. He was intrigued by her beauty and elegance. Her skin was the color of pecans, her eyes the color of cinnamon, and her lips were full. She was about 5'4", and what most men would consider thick in the hips and thighs. Her hair was cut in a layered bob that accented her facial features. When he heard her voice, which was majestic and charming, he knew that his pleasure would be derived from hearing her speak his name in the most intimate manner possible.

In less than three months, Donovan fell in love with Jade and decided he wanted to share his life with her. Until his relationship with Jade, he'd never envisioned himself getting married. Jade made him feel and believe in infinite possibilities. She was simply amazing to him and everything he desired. She was charismatic with a strong sense of style, and she was strong-willed and independent by nature. She was a warm, passionate lover, and he marveled at being the recipient of her love.

The love that he and Jade shared was so strong and intense that it consumed them like a tsunami. After a year and eight months, things became strained, and Jade decided to end the relationship. Donovan attempted to call her several times, but she would not accept his calls. Finally, in desperation, Donovan stopped by Jade's apartment. Tia answered the door, but would not allow him to enter. She told him that Jade had been sick and that she didn't need any added stress. Tia apologized, but asked Donovan to leave. In an effort to comfort him, she told him that Jade would be fine.

He sent her favorite flowers and a card. In the card, he asked Jade to call him if she needed anything. Jade eventually called Donovan and thanked him for his sincere tokens of concern. She assured him that she was doing well.

During their last conversation, he said, "*I love you. I only want what's best for you, even if you think it's not me. I will always be here."*

Several years later, Donovan heard that Jade dated and married Jonothan McNeir, Tia's older brother. He was told that she was happy and that her inner light had returned. For this he had been thankful, as her happiness had always mattered to him.

After his time with Jade ended, Donovan began dating Asia. They dated for three years and married. Asia was his love mate, but she was not his soul mate. He loved her, but there was something that restricted Donovan from giving himself wholeheartedly to his Asia. They shared eight years together filled with happiness and two years full of heartache and trials. Asia was a loving wife and phenomenal person. Her heart's desire was to become a mother. Unfortunately, Donovan and Asia were unable to have children of their own. With all the wealth that he had accumulated, Donovan could not give his wife her one desire, the miracle of conceiving a child. After several failed attempts, she accepted this reality and adoption became their only option.

Asia struggled emotionally for a year from situational depression. She and Donovan attended counseling for six months of that year to address Asia's insecurity concerning her infertility. Donovan did everything in his power to provide Asia with love and emotional support during this time. After regaining a sense of normalcy, Asia agreed to adoption. However, during the final stage of adopting Kamia and Kamill, their plans were altered. As peacefully as Asia had entered his life, she left it, passing away in her sleep. The autopsy report listed the cause of death as a ruptured brain aneurysm, but to Donovan, Asia died from a broken heart and spirit.

A gentle breeze brushed Donovan's face and he reacquainted himself with his surroundings, before his mind drifted back to his previous thoughts.

In spite of the turmoil going on in his life and the unforeseen challenge of being a single father, Donovan continued with the adoption process for Kamia and Kamill. The twins were three years old when the adoption was finalized.

A close family friend gave him a nanny's name and number. He interviewed Ms. Evelyn and hired her as a full-time nanny. Ms. Evelyn was widowed after thirty years of marriage, and with no family of her own, she instantly became an integral part of Donovan's family. The girls called her Granny Evelyn. She was attentive and gentle with the girls, a great cook, and not afraid to keep Donovan in check from time to time. She had been a part of their family for five years, and he was grateful for her.

With the support of Ms. Evelyn, his parents, and his sister Danielle, Kamia and Kamill were well-rounded little girls. Both girls excelled in their academics, athletics, and music. Now, at the age of eight, both girls wanted a mom. Donovan tried to love them enough for two parents, but Kamill's words echoed in his ears, "Little girls need more than just a daddy. We need a mommy." After Asia's death, Donovan dated other women. He had been set up by friends and family more times than he cared to recall. No woman seemed good enough for him or his girls.

Now, seeing Jade fourteen years after losing her, Donovan was overwhelmed with emotions. Although their paths had led them in different directions in the past, the love that he carried for her never changed or faded. It was simple in his mind...he wanted Jade. She needed him and the girls, and she would complete their family. In reality, a place outside of his mind and his heart, he knew that it would not be that simple. But Donovan would not give up his second chance to give Jade the love that he had tucked away in his heart.

"Thank you, God," Donovan whispered.

*****

Later that afternoon, Jade returned to the beach for an evening walk, listening to the songs from Tamela Mann's *Best Days* CD. Her mood was lighter. She looked around at the wonders of nature and the faces of strangers. She smiled and silently thanked God for her life. Jade stopped walking, closed her eyes beneath her shades, and took a deep breath.

As she was about to resume walking, she heard a woman's voice yelling, "Girls, watch where you are going. Stop running! Be careful…Kamill!"

Jade felt an impact, then cold as she hit the sandy beach on her left side. "Oh! Cold! Oh, oh!" Jade squealed, looking down to see a banana split covering her coral tunic and lower legs.

Beside her in the sand lay the cutest little girls with wide, hazel colored eyes. They were identical twins with beautiful, sable brown faces, doe shaped eyes, and button noses. Their soft locks were pulled back into ponytails with little ringlets framing their faces. They were about seven or eight years old.

Jade smiled at the children in spite of the ice cream running down her body. She could tell that one little girl was on the verge of tears. Jade helped them up off of the beach sand.

"I'm sorry, I didn't mean to…," one of the twins said.

"We're sorry; it was an accident," the other twin said, intertwining her fingers with her sister.

"It's okay, I know it was," Jade responded in an assuring tone. "Are you both okay?"

"Yes."

"Kamill Amari Johnson!"

"Kamia Aniya Johnson!"

Jade watched as the little girls flinched.

"Ma'am, I apologize." The older woman paused to catch her breath. The woman was tall and beautiful with strong feminine facial features accented by her short-cropped salt and pepper hairstyle. She was dressed in a burnt orange, one piece bathing suit with an African-print sarong.

"Hello, my name is Evelyn; these are my granddaughters, Kamia and Kamill."

"Hello, my name is Jade. It's nice to meet you, Ms. Evelyn, and you too, girls," Jade said with a smile.

"Granny, we tripped."

"They did. It was an accident," Jade interjected.

"But, *little girls*, didn't I tell both of you not to run?"

Jade turned her face to the side to hide her smile. Her mom and aunts used a similar tone when they called her *little girl* as a child and even at times as an adult.

"Yes ma'am," both girls responded in low voices.

"Now, have you apologized to this nice lady?" Ms. Evelyn looked at Jade.

"They did apologize. It's okay. Accidents happen," Jade responded.

"Well yes, they do. I apologize again. We will pay for your tunic to be dry-cleaned," Ms. Evelyn offered.

"That isn't necessary. I think I'm going into the water to wash away the ice cream. Is it okay for the girls to come in with me?"

Kamia and Kamill smiled.

"Well, okay. Girls, really quick, we need to head home and get ready for dinner. Jade, would you like for me to hold your phone?" Ms. Evelyn said, extending her hand to Jade.

"Yes, thank you. Okay, girls, let's hurry, but no running."

Ms. Evelyn sat and watched Jade and the girls submerge themselves into the water. She silently prayed for the young lady with sadness lurking in her eyes. She believed wholeheartedly that God did not allow accidental encounters.

As Jade and the girls returned, Ms. Evelyn handed them the beach towels she carried.

"Jade, would you like to join us for dinner?" Ms. Evelyn sensed Jade's hesitation, but continued. "Well, I know it's short notice, so how about lunch tomorrow? Here is our phone number; think about it."

Jade took the piece of paper and glanced at the number. "Thank you for the invitation. I'll call you later to let you know," Jade said as she handed the towel back to Ms. Evelyn.

"Alright, girls, let's go. Jade, we hope to hear from you."

Jade gathered her things and headed to Tia's house. When

she entered the house, the phone was ringing. She knew that it was her mother, Pearl Michaels. Her mom was extremely concerned for her emotional and physical well-being. She offered to come along, but Jade needed this time alone. So, to assure herself of her daughter's sanity, Pearl called Jade three times a day. Yes, it was annoying, but they set a call schedule around Jade's normal routine. The first call of the day was at 9:30 a.m., after her run on the beach. The second call was at 2:00 p.m., and the last call was around 7:30 p.m.

"Hi, Mom."

"Hi. Sweetie, I can hear you smiling over the phone. What has you sounding so delighted?" her mom asked.

Jade's smile widened as she thought about the intuitive woman her mom was.

"I just met the cutest little girls, Kamill and Kamia, on the beach. They both ran into me, with their banana splits falling all over us. They were apologetic, and their grandmother invited me to have lunch with them tomorrow."

"Really, are you planning to go?" Pearl asked.

"I think so. They were so sincere in their apology. I wouldn't want to offend them."

"Look, sweetie, you be careful. Okay?"

"Yes, Mom, I will. I love you and I'll talk to you later," Jade said.

*****

Later that night around 8:00 p.m., as Jade looked at paint and fabric samples, she thought to call Ms. Evelyn.

"Hello, Ms. Evelyn, this is Jade; we met today," Jade said.

"Oh yes. How are you, dear? I hope that you are calling to accept our lunch invitation for tomorrow."

"Yes, I am. What time should I come over? Oh, and I'll need directions," Jade said.

Ms. Evelyn was delighted that Jade accepted the lunch invitation. She gave Jade the time and directions. Ms. Evelyn always believed that food was nourishment to the body and the soul, and she was happy she could ensure that Jade had a home-cooked meal. She thought Jade was too thin.

"My, my, that child can't weigh more than 125 pounds wet! Yes, she needs a good meal," she said, searching the refrigerator and the pantry for menu ideas for their lunch date.

"Do you need anything from the market? I can go by and pick up any items for you," Donovan said as he entered the kitchen.

"Yes, I will. Here's a list. We are having a guest for lunch tomorrow," Ms. Evelyn said, not offering any additional information.

Donovan noted that Ms. Evelyn did not mention the name of the guest, the time, or the attire for the lunch. Translation: *your presence is not required.*

Chapter Two

J ade woke up shivering, holding her stomach as the memory of that night haunted her mind and heart. The dream always seemed so real.

In her dream, Jade and Jonothan shared dinner with his parents and were driving home. They were laughing about the looks on his parents' faces when they said that they didn't want to know the sex of the baby until birth. His parents had a difficult time adjusting to the fact that he and Jade were not following tradition. Jonothan's father was anxious to find out if he was having a grandson. His mother was upset because they would have to decorate the nursery in gender-neutral colors. His mother yelled, "This is our first grandchild! How dare you make us wait to know the sex of our grandchild!"

Jade and Jonothan's laughter turned into screams when they saw headlights and felt the impact from another car. Jade yelled as the car spun and then flipped. She could feel weight on her legs and heard the distant moans of her husband. She looked to her left and right, but could not see him. She yelled his name, but only heard more moans. He whispered her name before taking his last breath. Jade experienced an excruciating pain in her heart and then in her abdomen. "OH GOD! OH GOD, MY BABY!"

Her life had been forever changed by a drunk driver.

Jade took several deep breaths and got up from the bed. She washed her face with cold water over and over to ward off the tears that were pooling in her eyes. She looked at the clock and saw it was 4:48 a.m. She decided that it was not too early for her morning run.

As she ran, Jade prayed for relief from her broken heart and the grief that consumed her life for the past three years. It was a grief so strong that each passing day seemed like a lifetime, a grief so strong that even thoughts of her and her husband's happy moments caused her to hyperventilate.

Grief grasped her so strong, she could not free herself. Jade fought to control her emotions. Then, like a dam, the floodgates of her heart released the pain. Jade began to weep.

When she came to herself, she realized she had run several miles farther than her normal route. She was exhausted and didn't see a beach house nearby, so she started to walk back in the direction she had come. She walked about a mile and a half when she saw the first house. Suddenly, her vision became blurred and she felt lightheaded. Jade stumbled; each step seemed heavier, each breath labored. She whispered, "Oh God, help me."

*****

"Daddy! Daddy! We have to help her!" Kamill yelled, tossing and turning in her sleep. Her eyes opened and Donovan knew from the look in her eyes that the dream felt real. Kamill had a gift of dreams.

He asked, "What do we need to do?"

"It's the lady from the beach yesterday. The one we dropped ice cream on. I don't know her name, but I know where she is. Daddy, we have to go now. There's no one to help her. It's almost too late; we have to hurry." Kamill took off running out the door in her white nightgown and flip flops. Donovan was right beside her.

Kamill spotted Jade first. She yelled and pointed, "Hurry, Daddy! There she is!"

Donovan's first instinct was to reach for his daughter to keep her from running towards the woman.

*****

Jade saw a small figure running towards her and felt a sense of relief. She saw the silhouette of a man behind the girl and knew that she would be safe. She opened her mouth to yell for help, but it came out as a whisper. Jade staggered toward the figures until she felt her body waver. She was exhausted physically, mentally, and emotionally. Willing her mind, she opened her mouth and yelled, "Help me, please," before she passed out and darkness engulfed her.

*****

As Donovan approached the woman, a chill ran down his spine. It was Jade. His arms embraced her as she fell. The words "help me" had only escaped her lips moments before. Donovan was consumed with fear as he scooped her up into his arms and jogged towards the house.

Kamill ran ahead of Donovan to notify Ms. Evelyn. Ms. Evelyn and the girls waited on the porch.

"Donovan, what happened? Is that…? " Ms. Evelyn gasped and covered her mouth with her hand.

"Do you know her?" He asked.

"Yes! What happened?"

Donovan explained the scene on the beach. Ms. Evelyn began giving instructions to Donovan and the girls. A retired trauma nurse, she always traveled with medical supplies in case of an emergency.

Donovan laid Jade on the sofa. Ms. Evelyn tried several times to wake Jade without success. She checked her pulse.

"While I check her temperature, Donovan, go run a bath of room-temperature water and quickly come back. I'll need your help undressing her and getting her into the water. Kamill and Kamia, fill five Zip-lock bags with ice and place them in the bathroom sink."

Donovan carried Jade to his bathroom. He held her while Ms. Evelyn undressed her.

"Donovan, you will have to get in the tub and hold her up. I have to get the ice packs."

Donovan stood rooted to the spot. His legs would not allow him to move.

"Now, Donovan. Right now!" Ms. Evelyn spoke with authority.

Donovan did as he was told. He didn't realize he was holding his breath until Jade was secure in his arms. He took a breath and silently prayed for the woman he wanted to share the rest of his life with. Donovan concentrated on the task, not on the beautiful, naked woman before him. His thoughts were interrupted by Ms. Evelyn's voice.

"Her pulse is low and her body temperature is 102. I am going to place the ice packs under her neck, arm pits, and kneecaps. We need to get her body temperature down, without sending her body into shock. I am going to prepare the guest room for her. I'll be back to help you dry and dress her," Ms. Evelyn said, retreating from the bathroom.

Donovan couldn't imagine the depth of Jade's grief after burying a spouse and a child at the same time. After finding her on this island, he wanted nothing more than to love and care for her. He wasn't sure how all this would play out, but he wanted Jade in his life. He held her and prayed for them both.

Ms. Evelyn returned to the bathroom. "Once we have her in the bed, I'll call Dr. Morris to start an IV. She appears to be dehydrated and undernourished. Her body is exhausted. She is going to need plenty of fluids and rest for at least three to four days."

After Jade's body temperature decreased to 99, Donovan removed her from the bath. He dried and dressed Jade in one of Ms. Evelyn's large nightgowns and carried her to the guest room. Dr. Morris had already arrived by then and immediately started the IV. Once Ms. Evelyn had Jade settled into bed, she allowed the girls to come into the room and listen to her read the Bible.

Donovan excused himself to call Tia. He thought about the scars he saw on Jade's body from the car accident. She had lost so much. He knew that Jade had been eight months pregnant when the accident occurred.

"Tia, we found Jade collapsed on the beach this morning. I think that she'd been running. Dr. Morris said she'll be fine in a couple of days. I know, I know, I'll arrange your flight so you can come out here. Can you get to Atlanta Hartsfield-

Jackson International Airport by four o'clock? I agree that you should call her family, but wait until after you see her. That way you can better answer Ms. Pearl and Onyx's questions. Okay. I'll see you in a few hours."

*****

Donovan sent his private plane and Tia landed safely at McKinnon Airport in St. Simons at five o'clock. Tia smiled as Donovan approached her with open arms.

"Tia, she's okay. Ms. Evelyn is caring for her. She's receiving fluids to keep her hydrated. She thinks Jade is physically and emotionally exhausted."

Donovan loaded Tia's luggage and helped her into his Expedition. After they were settled into their driving route, Tia spoke first.

"Jade is exhausted. She has worked non-stop for the past three years to expand Holly Health to include community housing, as a memorial to Jonothan. We're all so worried about her."

When they arrived at the house, Donovan led Tia to the guest room, but neither entered. The door was ajar, and they could hear Ms. Evelyn's and Jade's voices.

"Mom," Jade whispered in a weak and raspy voice. Jade was disoriented and talking in her sleep.

"Yes, dear," Ms. Evelyn responded, not wanting to wake Jade or for her to become hysterical.

"Mom, I know you're concerned. But, I'm healing. Today, I opened my mouth, and for the first time in three years, prayers and praise flowed freely from my lips to God's ears. God gave me the strength to free myself from the grief that held me captive for all this time." Tears began to flow from Jade's eyes and she talked through her sobs. "I opened my eyes today and for the first time in a long time I saw and felt God's wonders, the color of the ocean and sky… the ocean breeze on my face and the arms of the angel He sent to me. My heart is healing."

24

Jade felt a hand caressing her face, wiping her tears.

"Shhh shhh, precious, just rest," Ms. Evelyn said. She was very concerned for Jade and wondered what this beautiful young woman was healing and running away from. A smile etched her face as she thought about Jade's reference to Donovan's arms. Ms. Evelyn noticed how Donovan held Jade as if she were familiar to him.

Ms. Evelyn needed to check on the girls. She quietly left the room and was startled by Tia and Donovan's presence in the hallway, but greeted Tia with a hug and a smile. From the moment Tia met Ms. Evelyn at the girls' school, she had observed her motherly spirit.

"How are you, dear?"

"I am well. How is Jade?" Tia asked.

"She is dehydrated and exhausted. She needs to rest for the next three to four days. She will be in and out of consciousness, but that's normal. I've prepared a room for you. Donovan, please bring Tia's luggage up and put it in the guest room at the end of the hall. Tia, you can go sit with her. She needs to know someone is near. If she starts talking, just listen and respond as she needs you to. Do you understand?" Ms. Evelyn said, looking from Donovan to Tia.

"Yes, ma'am," Tia replied humbly, and smiled.

Ms. Evelyn made a mental note to ask Donovan questions about the connection between him, Jade, and Tia, later. But for now, she would pray for physical healing, spiritual healing, and soul healing for Jade, Donovan, and Tia.

Tears sprang up in Tia's eyes as she stood at Jade's bedside. Jade looked so tired and vulnerable. Tia wasn't strong enough to help Jade through this alone. She stepped to the bay window, sat down, and dialed the number from memory.

"Hello, Onyx. Jade had a little accident, but she is fine. Please have Ms. Pearl pick up the other phone line. I want to tell you both what's going on."

Tia explained everything to Onyx and Ms. Pearl. After Tia explained everything, Onyx planned to request emergency leave and fly over as soon as she could. Ms. Pearl decided that she needed to come to St. Simons immediately.

"Ms. Pearl, I have a friend who is working on the flight arrangements for you. I'll call you back with the details." Tia ended the call and said a silent prayer.

She found Donovan in his home office. "Donovan, I talked with Onyx and Ms. Pearl. Ms. Pearl wants to come to St. Simons. I told them that I had a friend who was working on the flight arrangements."

"I've already made the arrangements. I scheduled Ms. Pearl's flight to arrive the day after tomorrow. I'll schedule my flight to leave that morning. I have to go to North Carolina on business. I think it's best I'm not here when Jade wakes up. I am afraid of how she'll respond when she sees me. I'll call Ms. Evelyn while I'm gone to check on her."

"Thank you. I'll pick up Ms. Pearl from the airport," Tia said. "Donovan, I believe that all of this, our meeting at Kamia's IEP, Jade coming to St. Simon, and even you following her here is meant to be. Life is not always what we want it to be, but God's ultimate plan for our life is for our good."

"I know, but seeing her this way is hard," Donovan replied.

Tia left Donovan's office and went back to the room to sit with Jade. Jade was truly her best friend and she deserved happiness with no more tragedies.

Tia witnessed Jade's discovery of love with both Donovan and Jonothan. Donovan and Jade loved one another with every fiber of their being, but their relationship ended with so much sorrow. Tia thought of the day that she'd sent Donovan away from her and Jade's apartment. She had shaken her head with regret, but believed that God allowed everything to happen for a reason. Jade found love again with her brother, Jonothan. Jonothan's death had broken Jade's heart. How had this happened? Why had this happened?

Tia believed that the reason she crossed paths with Donovan was the answer to her many prayers for Jade. She smiled at the great lengths that Donovan was going through for Jade. It had been clear during their conversations months ago that Donovan still loved Jade. Tia also knew of the love that Jade still carried for Donovan in her heart.

Chapter Three

Ms. Pearl arrived two days after the incident. She expressed great thanks to Ms. Evelyn and Tia for caring for Jade, and looked forward to meeting the gentleman who had saved her daughter's life. However, Pearl was certain that he was the same Donovan who had stolen and kept part of her daughter's heart many years ago. She decided to act none the wiser to what she thought was going on, even though the situation had Onyx's and Tia's names written all over it.

Jade woke on the fourth day. She heard faint voices and opened her eyes to see the pretty little girls from the beach. They both ran from the room and returned with Jade's mom, Ms. Evelyn, and Tia. Jade couldn't find her voice, but she smiled at the love she felt. Ms. Pearl sat next to Jade on the bed as Ms. Evelyn positioned herself next to Jade on the opposite side of the bed.

"Shhh, shhh, don't try to speak; sip on this water first." Ms. Evelyn said, then explained the activities that led up to that day, with no mention of Donovan.

"Jade, would you like to sit up?" Ms. Pearl asked.

"Yes."

"Evelyn, help me please. Jade, slowly, baby...that's it," Ms. Pearl said as she propped pillows behind Jade's neck.

"Okay, I want you to sit up in the bed for about fifteen minutes then we'll move you to the side of the bed. Then we'll move to the chair to eat," Ms. Evelyn said.

"Girls, Tia, please help me in the kitchen. We can warm Jade's soup and make her some tea. Let's leave Jade and Ms. Pearl alone for a few moments," Evelyn instructed. "Pearl, I'll go call Dr. Morris and when I get back we'll move Jade to the chair."

"Jade, Ms. Evelyn is your guardian angel," Ms. Pearl said. "I am thankful that she was here to take care of you."

"Mom, I'm sorry that you had to leave Hawaii," Jade said.

"Jade, hush. You're my daughter."

"Tia's here, Mom."

"Well Tia isn't as strong as she pretends to be. She called me and Onyx in tears and was very worried about you. Onyx would be here, but her leave request wasn't approved. She has called non-stop, checking on you since I arrived. I'll call her now.

"Onyx, your sister is awake; I'm putting you on speaker phone."

"Jade, if you wanted Mom to come back to Georgia, all you had to do was ask," Onyx said. "You didn't have to go and pass out on a beach. You've always been good for the theatrics."

"Onyx," Ms. Pearl chastened.

Jade laughed, and then coughed.

"Mom, she knows I'm joking. Jade, you scared me."

"I scared me too," Jade responded.

"Listen, I would be there if I could. I have to go into a meeting. I'll call you later this evening. I love you. Love you, Mama."

"I love you too, Onyx," Jade said.

"Me too, baby," Ms. Pearl said as she hung up the phone. "Jade, you listen to me," she continued. "I want to talk to you. It's time for you to. . ."

Jade interrupted her mother's words, "I'm getting better. I don't feel like there is a stone resting on my chest anymore," Jade looked around the room and smiled. "There is a calmness that resides here. It's like a kindred spirit is here and I feel safe. I am so thankful that Ms. Evelyn and the girls found me."

"We are too. Now, get up out of that bed," Tia said lightheartedly as she returned to the room with Jade's soup and tea.

Soon afterward, Jade finished eating, Dr. Morris arrived and advised that Jade drink plenty of fluids, and eat light before resuming a normal diet and physical activity.

Chapter Four

It had been exactly eight days since Jade collapsed. She felt rejuvenated and more focused. Jade, her mother, and Tia returned to Tia's home the day after she woke up. Tia returned to Atlanta with a promise to come back to St. Simons Island in two weeks. Jade and her mother were enjoying their time together as well as the company of Ms. Evelyn and the girls.

It was a Saturday, and the girls were spending the day on Jekyll Island with their father. Jade thought that it was strange that she had not met the girls' father yet, but hoped she would soon get the chance to meet and thank him.

Jade, her mom, and Ms. Evelyn treated themselves to a day at the spa. They returned, renewed, and enjoyed a wonderful lunch that Ms. Evelyn prepared for them.

Jade was clearing the table when the back door opened.

"We're back!" Kamia yelled.

Jade looked up into familiar eyes and gasped. It was Donovan, her first love. A range of bittersweet emotions consumed Jade as she looked at him in disbelief. She swayed and had to grip the table to steady herself. Instinctively, Donovan took two protective steps toward her.

Fortunately, the girls reached Jade first. Kamill and Kamia greeted her with chatter and hugs. Their touch sent warmth throughout her body, stabilizing her emotions. They pulled Jade towards a chair at the table, still chattering. Then, as if looking at Jade for the first time, they both touched her flushed face.

"Are you ok?" they asked.

"Yeah I'm ok. I'm just surprised. Tell me about your day," Jade responded as she pulled their little hands from her cheeks and held them. Jade held them until they both started talking again and needed their hands for gesturing.

"Girls, one at a time," Ms. Evelyn said gently. Her voice was so light that Jade was sure the girls hadn't heard her, but they did.

Kamia, usually more introverted, led the conversations about their day's adventure. "We walked on the beach and collected sea shells, starfish, and sand dollars."

Kamill chimed in, "Then we took a ferry boat ride to Jekyll Island and had the shells, starfish, and the sand dollars made into necklaces. See! Now look at mine."

"They're pretty," Jade smiled.

"We had one made for you. Daddy, where's the necklace for Ms. Jade?" Kamia said.

"Daddy? Please help her put it on," Kamill said.

Donovan waited for a nod or a smile from Jade that his daughters' request was okay.

"Daddy, please put Ms. Jade's necklace on her," Kamia squealed.

"Jade, look at what Donovan, Kamia, and Kamill had made for you," Ms. Pearl said. "Darling, it is simply beautiful. The shells have a blue tint. Girls, did you know blue is Jade's favorite color?" Ms. Pearl gently removed the necklace from Donovan's hands.

"It's pretty. Look in the mirror, Ms. Jade," the girls replied in unison as they pulled Jade to the wall mirror.

"It is beautiful. Thank you, Kamia, Kamill, and…Donovan. Thank you very much."

Jade couldn't control her voice. He always had that effect on her.

Based on the energy in the room, Ms. Evelyn thought to herself, "Donovan and Jade have shared time and space before." She inwardly questioned if their crossing of paths was divine destiny or if it had been a set up. She knew Donovan and thought the latter.

She smiled, knowing that God would still have the ultimate say. Love was the energy in the room. Plain and simple and to the native eye, love engulfed and transcended between Donovan and Jade. Her talk with Pearl would be very interesting tonight.

"Ms. Evelyn, the girls, and I are going to pick up a few things from Publix supermarket for dinner," Jade's mom yelled. "Jade, help Donovan clean the kitchen. We'll be back soon!"

Ms. Evelyn winked at Pearl and they all disappeared through the door.

It felt like a dream. Donovan was a vision of male perfection. At 6'3" and 250 lbs, his presence was totally overwhelming. He was handsome: his skin was the color of milk chocolate, his signature bald head and goatee, and his sable eyes. The specks of gray hairs in his goatee added more character to his already distinguished features. Donovan wore a white Polo T-shirt, khaki cargo shorts, brown dock-sider shoes, and a thin yellow gold Figaro chain with a K charm. Jade's body awakened from its three-year hibernation and desire surged through her. Her body responded, as it always had to the man who stood in front of her.

Donovan couldn't control the rapid race of his heartbeat or his body's immediate response to Jade. She looked majestic... Her hair was loose, curled in tendrils. She smelled of lemongrass and sage and was wearing a sleeveless, sheer lavender shirt that exposed a white tank top, with white linen pants, flat silver thong sandals, and a rose gold necklace with two miniature birthstone booties.

Before Jade or Donavan could speak, they both leaned into one another. He rested his forehead on hers. She placed her hands flat on his chest. They stood there together, eyes closed, until their breathing and heartbeats synchronized. Then she rested her head on his chest. He wrapped his arms around her and held her close.

Jade became completely lost in the moment and her spirit smiled. Her mind drifted back to a time when he was the love of her life. A familiar melody by Zhane began to play in Jade's mind: "*...If music was love, the thought of you would always make me sing, la, la , la, la, la, la.*"

Jade looked up into his sable-colored eyes and they held

each other's gaze. At that moment, she visited a place deep inside her heart that she had locked away. It was a secret place full of love and hurt that was too unbearable to visit often. Jade closed the door and relocked her secret place to rejoin Donovan in this space of time, and the melody faded. Donovan felt Jade's body fill with tension. Instinctively, he released her and stepped away, but only after he placed a gentle kiss on her forehead.

"Ms. Evelyn will expect the kitchen to be spotless. I'll wash and you rinse."

Donovan and Jade worked quietly and efficiently for the next ten minutes. They functioned like a well-oiled machine, their rhythms naturally in sync. Jade rinsed, dried, and Donovan put the dishes up without much effort.

"You've made quite an impression on my girls. They adore you. They've talked about you nonstop since you met on the beach."

"They are wonderful kids. You should be very proud."

"Thank you, I am."

Jade finally asked, "How long have you known I was here?"

"I carried you to the house from the beach. You were so sick. Not just your physical body, but your spirit seemed broken, too. I didn't want you to see me until you were well. I knew Ms. Evelyn and the girls would take good care of you until then. I called Tia and made the arrangements to fly her and your mom here. Then I flew out for a week on business. I arrived back two days ago." He pushed a tendril of hair from Jade's face.

His fingertips felt like velvet on her skin. Jade felt overwhelmed with emotions and her body spiraled from his touch.

"Jade, I…" he began.

"I better get back to the house, but before I go, I want to know if you, Tia, and Onyx…? Never mind," she said as she stepped away from Donovan.

He seemed aware of her anxiety, "Jade, let me walk you back to Tia's house."

"Donovan, I'm fine."

"No, you're not. Let's talk," he reached out and caressed her arm. She was trembling. "Jade."

"No, we'll talk later, okay?" Jade's eyes were locked with his and she couldn't move, she could barely breathe. "The girls and I were supposed to watch the *Princess and the Frog* tonight. I'm sorry, but I won't be able to," Jade said as she closed the screen door.

Her heart constricted and her insides were tangled in knots from the emotions that Donovan evoked within her. On the walk back to the house, Jade reminisced about the relationship she and Donovan had when they were younger.

Donovan and Jade first met when they were in college. Donovan had strolled into their nine o'clock English class looking like he had stepped off a cloud. He wore a white Polo shirt, khaki linen pants, brown shoes, and a brown belt. He was handsome and appeared to be a natural charmer. Although Jade was not looking to be in a relationship at the time, she could not help but be attracted to him. She could not ignore the magnetism she felt as he looked into her eyes as he walked passed her seat.

Donovan ran behind Jade as she walked to her next class. He grabbed her gently by the hand and asked her to slow down. "Excuse me, Miss. I am sorry. I couldn't help but notice you in our English class. What is your name?"

Jade blushed and told him her name.

"Your name is just as beautiful as you are. My name is Donovan. May I walk you to your next class?" Donovan asked.

Jade smiled and nodded yes.

Jade and Donovan talked and walked the entire time. She felt comfortable with him and was disappointed when she had to go into the classroom. He assured her that he would come back to pick her up once class was done. Jade walked into the classroom with a huge smile on her face.

Jade and Donovan's relationship blossomed. Jade received physical and emotional satisfaction from the relationship. She ultimately fell head over heels in love with him.

Donovan was a natural leader. His quick intellect, intuition, and alertness gave him an aura that intrigued Jade. He was confident and never doubted his ability to achieve his personal or academic goals. However, from time to time when Donovan experienced a disappointment, he would shut down and shut Jade out. Jade was not used to this and his behavior was a concern for her. Jade grew up in a house full of love and she believed in a fairytale love that required complete vulnerability. Shutting down emotionally or blocking others out had not been an option in her parent's home.

Jade's parents were high school sweethearts and wonderful people who adored one another. Her father was a Full Bird Colonel in the United States Army when he died. He represented everything that Jade believed a man should be. He was an alpha male: a provider, protector, and nurturer. He loved his wife and daughters with everything within him. Her parents taught her and Onyx that the foundation of life was God, family was valuable, open communication was important, and that love was the greatest gift. Their thoughts were synced and they could complete one another's sentences. Jade marveled at their love, she was aware that her parents existed together as one.

Jade loved Donovan and attempted to support him in every way. He was in many ways like her father. But as time passed in their relationship, she began to feel that her love for him consumed her entire being. Donovan talked about their life plans and timelines but not once did he request her input *on their life together.* Jade was also a natural leader, so relinquishing control of her life for love was an inward struggle. She began to fear that her desires, dreams, and opinions would be neglected or forgotten. She began to seek some control in her relationship with Donovan by becoming more vocal and challenging his way of thinking and his timeline. Her issues with control and Donovan's inability to compromise ultimately drove Jade to end their relationship.

Although she'd chosen to leave Donovan, her love for him and his love for her was never in question. After their breakup, Jade saw Donovan occasionally in passing until she graduated from college. However, after graduation, Jade had no further contact with Donovan, until today.

With time and Jonothan, Jade learned that love, real love, was enough. She understood and accepted that one's inability to compromise, along with other unconscious restrictions due to a lack of trust, hindered a stable foundation for a relationship to grow and sustain. With Jonothan, Jade learned to compromise and relinquish her desire for control in their relationship. She learned that loving, giving of her heart, and co-existing with another person was a privilege. It was a privilege to love Jonothan and to exist as one with him. The unconditional love they shared healed her heart.

Jade met Tia's brother, Jonothan when she and Tia were in college. Jonothan was six years Jade's senior. He was handsome and a genius-like level of intelligence and he was humble and kind. Jonothan was away at medical school and doing his residency. He interacted with Jade when he visited Tia on campus or during the holidays when Jade spent the time with Tia and her family.

It was during a three-week vacation in Myrtle Beach after she and Tia graduated from college that Jonothan openly expressed a romantic interest in Jade. He'd agreed to teach Jade to learn how to swim. Jonothan was patient, gentle, but firm and the reward was that at age 23 she learned to swim. In all of the excitement, Jade hugged Jonothan and he kissed her. From that moment, he "courted" her. He earned her love and trust.

Jade began to hum the lyrics to India Arie's "*He Heals Me*" as she thought of her late husband with ease. She reached for her cell phone, and then realized that she had left it on the kitchen table at Ms. Evelyn's . . . no, at Donovan's house. There was no way she was going back to get it. She would just have to call Tia when she reached the house.

Donovan being on St. Simons was not a coincidence, she thought. This was Tia and Onyx. How could they? Did her mom know? Of course, she knew. She knew everything.

Jade's mind raced with many thoughts. She heard the phone ringing when she reached the porch of the beach house. She was certain that one of the guilty parties were calling. She checked the caller ID and saw Onyx's name.

Jade answered calmly, "Yes, Onyx?"

There was a brief pause, mainly because Onyx was caught off guard by the calmness of Jade's voice.

"Jade?"

"Uh hum."

"Jade, stop the wheels in your mind from turning and listen, okay?"

Jade didn't speak. Onyx took it as a cue to continue and Jade quickly knew her suspicions were correct. Onyx and Tia had orchestrated her "reunion" with Donovan.

"We thought... there was no other way. You would have ever agreed. We want you to be happy, again." Onyx took a deep breath before she continued. "It's been three years. Jonothan would have wanted you to be happy. Jade, I would give anything to see *my man* again. We thought that you--"

Click! Jade ended the call. "WE...WE!!! Jonothan...What... man...she doesn't have a man! " Jade yelled to no one.

Jade stretched out across the bed and stared up at the ceiling. She ignored Onyx and Tia's continual calls to the house phone for more than twenty minutes. They both knew the love that she had for Jonothan and the depth of the love she shared with Donovan, but that didn't give them the right to. . . Her thoughts were interrupted by knocks at the door.

"Jade, it's Donovan."

"Donovan, what do you want?"

Jade, I brought your cell phone. Can we talk?"

"No. Please leave the phone on the table. I'll get it after you leave."

"I think we should talk. Please."

"D, just leave the phone."

"Okay. Goodnight."

After about an hour, Jade walked out to retrieve her phone and found her mother at the door.

"Jade Simone Michaels, sit down and listen," her mother said in a tone that dared Jade to defy her.

Jade did as she was told.

"Onyx and Tia both love you and want you to be happy. Although I don't agree with what they've done, they meant well. "

"They had no right," Jade said, never making eye contact with her mother.

"You've been stuck in grief for a long time, Jade. Look around you; it's time you open your eyes and live. God spared your life for you to live, not drown in your grief and sorrow. It's time that you entertain the thought of opening your heart to love. Whether you want to believe it or not, there is still something very strong between you and Donovan. It was evident to Ms. Evelyn, to me, and even to the twins. But I won't push or probe right now. I'll talk with Tia and Onyx."

"Please do," Jade said with irritation.

"I will, but right now you need to apologize to Kamill and Kamia. They were very disappointed that you missed movie night."

"Mom, I can't go over there."

"You don't have to go over there, but you can call. Children forgive easier than adults. They adore you, Jade. So fix this," her mom said in a stern voice.

Jade called to apologize to the twins, and they rescheduled movie night for the following evening at Tia's home instead of Donovan's.

Then, Jade called Tia.

"Tia, how could you!"

"Jade, I know you're upset," Tia responded calmly.

"Upset is not the word that I would use. I am livid! You and Onyx crossed the line this time."

"We always cross the line, Jade. You cross the line with us. That's what we do."

"Well you both went too far with this!"

"No, we didn't! Jade, you won't give yourself permission to move on. It's been three years. Jonothan was my brother. I know how much he loved you and how much you loved him. But I was there to witness the love you shared with Donovan, remember."

Silence. Tia imagined Jade pacing back and forth.

"Jade, I'm Kamia's speech therapist."

"What?"

"Yeah, Donovan came in for an IEP shortly after you decided to come to St. Simons. We met for dinner just to catch up. When he asked about you, there was a spark in his eye and a catch in his voice. Although, he owned his house on St. Simons already, he was hesitant to seek you out there. It took me and Onyx a few months to convince him to go for it."

"Jade, how did you feel when you saw him?" Tia asked quietly.

"That doesn't matter," Jade responded.

"Yes, it does."

"Tia, you and Onyx had no right."

"Jade, stand still, give yourself permission, and tell me what you felt when you saw him," Tia pleaded.

"I couldn't breathe."

"Why?"

"Because I was shocked! I couldn't believe it was him!"

"Stand still, Jade," Tia instructed. "Okay, let's put aside the fact that you were shocked. Be honest, how did you feel?"

"I couldn't breathe,"

"Jade Simone, you said that already. How did you feel?" Tia asked gently.

"I felt safe when he held me."

"He held you! Um hum! So, he held you. You can be livid, but soon you'll be thanking me."

"Tia!"

"Girl, please, I can't wait to say 'I told you so.' I'll call you tomorrow. Love ya! Bye."

Jade was left holding the phone with her mouth open. She laughed in spite of herself when she realized that Tia had hung up the phone.

The next day went by fast. Throughout the day, Jade considered canceling movie night with the twins, but she did not want to disappoint them again. Jade ordered pizza, wings, and drinks. Then she prepared small cups of vanilla ice cream and put them in the freezer. She set up the ice cream sundae bar with a variety of toppings for the girls to finish off their sundaes. As a small peace offering, Jade also set out Donovan's favorite ice cream, butter pecan.

When Jade opened the door for the girls, they shed their flip flops on the mat beside the door.

"My dad's coming. He is walking, but we ran ahead," Kamill said.

"He has cupcakes," Kamia said.

"That's great. I have vanilla ice cream for dessert and different toppings for you to choose from."

"We love vanilla ice cream, but our dad only eats butter pecan ice cream."

"I know. I bought butter pecan ice cream for him. Your dad and I were friends in college."

"Really!" Kamia said excitedly.

"Yep," Donovan interrupted as he walked into her house, placing the cupcakes on the kitchen counter.

Jade hadn't heard Donovan come in. She met his gaze, heat surged through her, and she quickly refocused on the girls. "Okay, let's get the movie ready while your dad fixes our plates."

Jade and Donovan exchanged looks throughout the night. Jade realized how comfortable she felt being around Donovan and the girls. She had to admit to herself that the something her mother was referring to was definitely there.

Chapter Five

Before Jade realized it, two weeks had passed. Her mom had settled in and was enjoying her vacation, too. She and Ms. Evelyn were social butterflies, always off enjoying something together. Jade's daily routine now included spending some time with Donovan and the girls.

Although a small town, Brunswick had character and activities for Kamill and Kamia. They went to the movies, skated, got pedicures and manicures, and shopped. They also rode their bikes, visited the Splash Island Water Park on Jekyll Island, built sand castles on the beach, and flew their kites.

Donovan was an awesome father and very attentive to both girls. He encouraged and challenged them to be their best. Kamia became more outspoken and lit up in her dad's presence.

Jade realized that she lit up in Donovan's presence, also. Tonight was the first evening that they shared alone. They talked and laughed about the girls, random topics, books, and movies as they walked along the beach. The stars were beautifully arranged in the sky and the moonlight was serene. Jade had no idea what the future held, but tonight she felt safe and light as a feather.

She reached for Donovan's hand and said, "I think that I should head back to the house."

"Alright, but first, make a wish upon a star."

"I already have," she responded.

They walked hand in hand back to Tia's beach house. When they reached the front steps, Donovan said, "I have enjoyed our time together. Thank you for making this trip memorable for Kamill and Kamia."

"I'm the one who should be thanking you for sharing your time and your daughters with me. You are a great father," Jade responded.

He stroked Jade's face. "I think you are an amazing woman

and my girls adore you. I have to go out of town for a week or so. I am flying to Denver Sunday morning for two days, then to North Carolina, but I will be back late on Saturday. Will you have dinner with me tomorrow night?"

"Yes," Jade whispered. She'd been so caught up in the whirlwind of the last two weeks that Donovan's work schedule had not crossed her mind.

"How does dinner and fun on the Pink Princess sound to you?"

"That sounds great."

"I'll pick you up at six. Good night." He kissed her on the forehead and left.

As Donovan walked back towards his home, he thought of the time he'd spent with Jade. The past two weeks had been a test of his will power, but today had been torture. They all had gone swimming together. Although she wore a modest bronze one-piece bathing suit with a multi-color wrap, Donovan knew every curve of her body. She was mesmerizing to him. He was looking forward to their date tomorrow night.

After Donovan left, Jade picked up the phone and nervously called Tia. As soon as Tia picked up the phone, Jade blurted out, "He invited me to dinner."

"What's the big deal? You've shared dinner with him a lot lately," Tia replied.

"I know, but the girls, mom, and Ms. Evelyn were there. This isn't the same."

"Oh, so you have a date, alone with Donovan. Where is he taking you?"

"Dinner and fun on the Pink Princess, and I don't have anything to wear."

"Jade, you're nervous? Okay, there's a little boutique in downtown Brunswick called Mary's Boutique. The owner is Mary Louise. She opens at 10 a.m. Go by first thing in the morning, just in case she has to make alterations."

"Thank you. Tia, I'm nervous. I feel things I haven't felt in years. Is it possible?"

"Yes, we both know that it's possible and it's okay. Go by Mary's and have fun tomorrow night. I love you, but I have to take this call."

Jade arrived at Mary's Boutique shortly after ten in the morning. Jade introduced herself to the owner, a beautiful, tall woman in her late fifties. "I just spoke with Tia," she told Jade. "She is such a sweet child. Come, Jade. Stand here,"

Mary looked at Jade and nodded. "Have a seat here and I'll be back," she said, walking away.

When Mary returned, she'd chosen three sexy dresses and a black linen strapless mid cafe-length romper.

"They would all look wonderful on you, but I think the black romper would be perfect. The dressing room is right through there. Try it on, while I pull your accessories together," Mary said before disappearing to the back of the store.

"I love it," Jade said, looking at herself.

Mary returned with accessories: a pair of three-inch, gray and black snakeskin sandals, with the matching clutch and the jewelry. Jade's attire was classy, sassy, and sexy.

*****

Wow was Donovan's first thought when Jade opened the door, but he could not speak. She looked stunning! How was he supposed to make it through the night with her looking so damn gorgeous? He closed his eyes and willed his body not to betray him.

"Donovan, are you okay?" Jade asked.

He opened his eyes and saw genuine concern on Jade's face.

"I am fine. I lost my voice at the sight of you. You look gorgeous."

In spite of herself, Jade felt white heat run through her body and settle at the core of her womanhood. She smiled, hoping to conceal the fire within her body.

"Thank you."

"We should leave before we're late," Donovan placed his hand on the small of Jade's back and they walked to his car, a black BMW.

Jade was excited as they drove to the pier. She had no idea what to expect that evening, but all that mattered was that she was spending it with Donovan. Jade and Donovan's fun began the moment they boarded the Pink Princess Casino boat. They were greeted by the Cruise Director, who directed them to the dining area. They enjoyed a romantic dinner, which included a salad and lobster, crab, and shrimp pasta.

After dinner, Jade and Donovan walked outside to the deck and enjoyed the breeze from the water. Both swayed to the music from the band.

"May I have this dance?"

"Yes, what took you so long to ask?" Jade teased.

"I'm nervous," he held her close and inhaled her scent.

"Why are you nervous?"

"I really want to impress you and we both know that my dancing is not the way to impress anyone."

They both laughed and Donovan took the opportunity to kiss Jade on the neck. To his surprise, she relaxed against his body even more. They danced closely until the band played an up-tempo song.

"Let's go inside to the casino," Donovan said.

"Okay, but I don't know how to play anything," Jade confessed.

"I'll teach you."

As Jade and Donovan entered the casino, both men and women stared at them. Donovan smiled with a sense of pride and pulled Jade closer to him. She looked up into his face and smiled.

Jade and Donovan played slots and other machines. She noticed that several women couldn't keep from glancing in Donovan's direction. Jade felt a sting of jealousy and found herself pressing her body closer to him or reaching for his hand as they walked through the casino.

"Donovan, what is the name of that game?" Jade asked, pointing to a table in front of them.

"That's roulette. You want to play?"

"Well.., maybe. Will you teach me how to play?"

Donovan gave Jade a quick tutorial on roulette and encouraged her to try it.

"I'll play, and then you can play," he said, seeing the apprehension on her face.

After the fifth game, Jade didn't appear to be as apprehensive. "Okay, babe, it's your turn. It's a numbers game, so just go with your instincts," he said, pulling her onto his lap. He knew that her sitting on his lap was against the rules, but it lightened her mood.

"D, move; you're making me nervous."

Donovan got up and stood behind Jade's chair. He offered no advice, not even when she looked to him. He would shrug his shoulders instead. She watched the board and went with her intuition as she played her favorite numbers: the twins' birthday and Donovan's birthday. To her surprise, she did well.

After winning $700, Jade got up from the roulette table and cashed in her winnings. She gave the money to Donovan because she didn't feel comfortable having that amount of money in her clutch. The remainder of the night, they danced, laughed, and enjoyed their time together.

The drive back to Tia's house was quiet; only the radio played as Jade and Donovan both reflected on their night together. Neither knew what to say, and were too afraid to say anything for fear that it would be the wrong thing. They didn't realize they both shared the same thoughts: "*Everything felt right, as if no time had passed. Why was it so easy?*"

After arriving at Tia's house, they held hands as he walked her to the door. Donovan finally spoke in a low voice. "I had a wonderful time."

"Me too," Jade responded.

"I don't want the night to end. I don't want to let you go."

Donovan paused to allow Jade to respond, but she didn't. He was sure that he'd said too much, too soon.

"Ms. Evelyn will forward you my itinerary for next week." He kissed her on the forehead and walked away.

Donovan had only taken four steps away from Jade when she called his name. He turned and walked back towards her. He pulled her into his embrace and found her lips, kissing her gently. He moaned at the feel of her lips, which were soft and featherlike. With the tip of his tongue, he touched her lips, outlining them slowly. The sensation caused Jade to sway. Donovan's arms tightened around her as the kiss changed from wanting a taste to needing a taste. He held her mouth captive. When Donovan released Jade's mouth, they both sighed with satisfaction.

He rested his head on hers and said, "Be sweet."

All Jade could say was, "Okay."

Donovan walked away knowing that the next few days would be hard. Although he was elated by his and Jade's reunion, he was now open to all the emotional roller coasters that were guaranteed to go with it.

Chapter Six

J ade sped down I-95 South back to St. Simons from Savannah, hoping that she hadn't missed Donovan's nightly call. She had been shopping at Home Goods for more accessories for Tia's house.

Jade thought of Donovan more and more as the days and nights passed. Jade felt things that she thought were impossible when she was with Donovan. She wasn't sure where they would go from this point, but she would allow her mind to wonder and her heart to feel.

Donovan had been gone close to a week. He text Jade periodically throughout the day and called in the evenings. Their conversations were delightful and enlightening as they talked about various topics ranging from world events to sports. He talked about himself and his life over the past fourteen years. He told Jade about his marriage and the love he shared with Asia, his adoption of Kamia and Kamill, and how Ms. Evelyn became a part of their family. More importantly, he shared special memories and quirky moments that he had with his daughters. Jade believed that it was those moments that added to the character of a person and enhanced their life. Donovan made a conscious effort to not ask Jade questions or encourage her to talk about the events of her life. She recognized and appreciated his thoughtfulness, and told him as much during their last conversation.

"Donovan, thank you for not pushing me to talk about my life with Jonothan and the accident."

"You're welcome. When you are ready to talk, I'll be here. There is no need to rush. I just found you, again," Donovan said with sincerity.

When she arrived at the house, she immediately checked the caller ID, but Donovan had not called. She was relieved that she hadn't missed his call. She looked around the room at the beautiful bouquet of flowers that he sent yesterday. The card read, "Roses are red, violets are blue, but lavender lilies are just for you." Jade unloaded the items she purchased, showered, and lay in the bed with the house phone at her side.

*****

Jade woke up at 2 a.m., startled from her dream. She had fallen asleep thinking of Donovan and awoke with him on her mind. Why hadn't he called? Jade chastised herself for being disappointed. It was not written in stone that they had to talk every night. Should she call him? No. It was too late. She decided to play it safe and text Tia instead, when she noticed a text message from Donovan. "Hey there, beautiful. I had a long day. I just woke up from a nap. I didn't want to startle you by calling. I'll call you in the morning. Sweet dreams and don't let the bed bugs bite."

She smiled and envisioned his face. For the first time in three years, another man had gently entered her thoughts and begun to re-open her heart.

An overwhelming feeling of guilt washed over her. The guilt demanded recognition and resolution. She needed closure on the part of her life that included Jonothan before she could pursue anything with Donovan.

Jade had only loved two men in her life, Donovan and Jonothan. One man she walked away from, too afraid of the love they shared. The other man she allowed herself to love, but he was taken away from her.

Despite the mixed emotions, Jade admitted to herself that she missed being loved and loving back. She missed companionship and holding hands. She missed being kissed and held by a man. She missed the intimacy of sharing her mind and body with the man she loved. At that moment, she decided to celebrate life and explore the new path before her. She smiled with contentment, snuggled deep into the covers, and fell back asleep, as the storm rains and winds played a melody outside.

*****

Mother Nature's aura the next morning was a sultry heat, with lingering remnants of the storm from the previous night. The rhythm of the continual rain was intoxicating. Jade had been humming along with the sultry tunes of Tamia, Alicia Keys, Fantasia, Faith, India Aire, Jill Scott, Ledsi, Mary J., Monica, and Tweet, since early morning. Her iPod was full of passionate, soul-stirring music, music that awakened desires only a man's touch or voice could satisfy.

Jade felt sensual and sexy, as her body throbbed with need, and visions of Donovan consumed her. Jade's mind reflected back through the years… she remembered the look and feel of his hands. His long, slender fingers had caressed and given her body insurmountable pleasure. His strong touch had always been gentle with love, desire, and a need for her. Back then, his hands had been slightly callused from working the night shift at the loading docks. After work, he would stop by his apartment to shower, change, and attend classes from 8 a.m. to 1 p.m. After class, he would drive to Jade's apartment. They would share lunch and talk before Jade left for her classes.

Donovan's sleeping patterns had always been unusual. He had never seemed to require a lot of sleep. While Jade was in class, Donovan usually rested. Although Jade would complain about Donovan invading her space with his clothes, workout bag, football, basketball, and other assorted items, there was comfort in knowing that he was waiting for her, in her bed, at her apartment.

Donovan was an amazing, selfless, and thorough lover. Time was never of concern for him. His kisses were intoxicating. He was not a verbal lover, but Jade could tell he enjoyed their intimacy as much as she did. She loved the sounds that escaped his lips when he entered her. It was a sweet low moan followed by a whisper of her name.

She inhaled…yes, she remembered his hands. When he would place his hand on the small of her back, it sent shivers down her spine to her womanly core and she would lose her breath. She always felt secure from him simply resting his hand on her or embracing her.

Regardless of what he needed from her physically or emotionally, she attempted to give it to him. Jade loved and adored Donovan with all her heart.

She could discern Donovan's emotional state from the way he initiated and made love to her.

When Donovan felt frustrated, he would snuggle close to Jade, as if seeking refuge and security. She would hold him, whispering "I love you" and other melodies of love to him. Donovan would initiate their lovemaking session without words and kisses. He would look deep into her eyes while stroking and stirring her fountain to life. After sheathing himself, he would position Jade atop him and she would fill herself with him. While she made love to him, they held each other's gaze. Jade would continue to whisper words of love to him as she searched his eyes for the source of his emotional state. Before his eyes betrayed him, he would reposition her hands and knees, then enter her from behind. He would love her body hard, as if trying to control and conquer it. Her body would surrender and withhold nothing from him. After their love session, they would shower together. He would bathe her and kiss her gently. When they returned to bed, he would spoon her and hold her tight. Still, he spoke no words.

When Donovan felt insecure or experienced an imbalance in his life, he initiated their love making session by whispering "I need you" and kissing her mindlessly. He would trail kisses over her body while telling her that he loved her over and over again. And then he would love her with his mouth until she erupted. He would sheath himself and position himself between her thighs, place her legs on his shoulders, and enter her with one long, hard stroke. He would love her hard and deep. While still connected, he would reposition the soles of her feet flat on his chest. He would look into Jade's eyes, as if willing her to surrender by saying his name and telling him that her loving was only for him. And yes, she always complied. It was after those times that he would stroke her back and say, "I love you and I appreciate you. Thank you for loving me."

Jade and her thoughts were interrupted and forced back to the present by the lyrics of Maxwell's "Sumthin." Jade picked up the phone, hesitated, and ended the call. Then she picked up the phone again. Donovan had called her earlier that morning. They talked for about thirty minutes. *I just need to hear his voice, again,* she thought.

Donovan's voice was strong and masculine. Jade prepared a little explanation for the call, but it went directly to his voicemail. She smiled as she listened to his outgoing message. Although he did not answer, her craving to hear his voice was satisfied. Jade did not leave a message. She knew that once he noticed the missed call that he would call her back. Her plan was simple; she would not answer the call. There was no reason for him to know that she was experiencing a momentary setback of emotions.

Jade was sitting at the table when her cell phone buzzed a familiar tune…Tamia's "Almost." She smiled, took a deep breath, deviated from the plan, and answered.

"Hey, sweetheart, what's going on?" Donovan said.

Donovan's term of endearment, "sweetheart," caught Jade off guard and she couldn't find her voice.

"Jade, what's up? Is everything okay? Say something or I'm on my way to the airport."

"Everything's okay. I was able to get what I needed without speaking directly to you," she responded.

"Babe, that's great, but I still would like to know why you called, humor me, please."

Complete silence.

"Jade Simone Michaels," he said her full name through clenched teeth.

"Donovan, I don't want to mislead you, but I wanted… well…" Be honest, an inner voice whispered. "I needed to hear your voice. Listening to your outgoing message was sufficient."

"Hmmm. Well, this is interesting. You are flirting with me."

"No, no, don't make this out to be more than it is. I'm not flirting," she giggled. "Oh my gosh, I am a thirty-six year-old woman, giggling," she said to herself.

"Jade, I repeat, you are flirting with me," he said with humor in his voice.

"I'm not. I just needed to hear your voice and I did. Thank you very much. My telling you about it is not flirting."

"Okay, babe, whatever you say."

"No, don't do that. I am not flirting. I'm being honest...I needed to hear your voice again this morning."

"So you had to be thinking of me."

"Yes, nothing specific. Just random thoughts," she responded, with a smile as wide as the Sahara desert.

"Well, at least you are thinking of me and admitting it. That's progress."

"No. I told you at the beginning of this conversation that I did not want to mislead you. It's nothing...we can't just go back...I can't. I can't explain; it's one of those days for me. My emotions are all over the place. Let's just take one day at a time. I'm still feeling my way with you."

"Jade, okay. Thank you for being honest with me. Now, it's my turn to be honest with you. I know we can't just pick up where we left off fourteen years ago. But, I need you. And you just expressed out loud your need for me. Today your need was only for the sound of my voice. I can only hope that each day brings more yearning until you need me, until you want me."

His voice became huskier and his breathing changed as he said, "I hope for more yearning until you need to feel my embrace, until you need to feel my hands touching you, until you need my kisses to satisfy your craving, and until you need to feel me deep inside of you, loving you with all that I am. Jade, I am not afraid to admit to you or myself that I want and need you in my life. I love you and I'll see you this evening."

Then the call was disconnected.

Donovan brushed his hand down his face and leaned forward. "Damn it!" He said I love you too soon. He sensed the hesitation in her voice during their conversation. "I've scared her. I said too much, too soon. We broke up in college because I didn't talk enough, now I'm talking too much. Even now at thirty-eight, Jade is still keeping me unbalanced." Donovan sighed. "But I want her back."

He thought about something that his grandfather told him once, "A woman will marry a man that she can live with. But a man, a real man, will only marry the woman he can't live without."

Donovan had lived without Jade for fourteen years. *No more*, he vowed. Being able to love the woman made just for him was a privilege he would not relinquish again.

Donovan reflected on his relationship with Jade in college. He'd loved her at first sight. Then once he'd gotten to know her, he believed that they would marry, have kids, and live the American Dream. Donovan grew up in a home full of love and strong family values. Donovan's grandfather had been the patriarch of the family, and the CEO of Johnson and Johnson, LLC. Donovan worked beside his grandfather and father most of his teen years with the understanding that one day he would assume responsibility for his family's financial consulting firm. It was this ambition that fueled Donovan to work so hard in college to achieve.

Donovan's mind traveled between the past and present for most of the day to identify the previous challenges of his and Jade's relationship. He reflected on the person that he was and the person that he'd become. He hoped that the person he was now would be enough for Jade.

"Donovan, look at me," Gavin, his coworker, said. He had been standing in front of Donovan's desk unnoticed for at least two minutes. "Hey, man. What is going on with you? D, this is a multimillion-dollar deal and your mind is not here."

"Man, you don't have to remind me about this deal, I set it up. It's Jade," Donovan said with a defeated tone.

"Have you told her how you feel?" Gavin asked.

"Yes, but I'm having a hard time adjusting to the uncertainty between us. She's still amazing and I want her to share my world. But what if she isn't open to exploring a relationship with me?"

"D, give her time. You knew that she would need time when you started planning all this."

"You're right." Unable to concentrate and lacking motivation, Donovan chose to end his business trip early. "Look, I need to head back to the island tonight. Gavin, can you finish up everything this afternoon by 3 p.m.?"

"Okay... 3 p.m., no problem," Gavin replied.

Although Donovan didn't require much sleep, his nights and days had been preoccupied with thoughts of Jade. He decided to head upstairs to his studio apartment for a nap before his flight to St. Simons. Donovan took a hot shower and drank a cold glass of chocolate milk to help him rest. Donovan's attempt to rest soon became a dream of Jade. He woke with the anticipation of seeing her.

Chapter Seven

Shortly after her conversation with Donovan, Jade decided to take a break from adding the finishing touches to Tia's house. She fell asleep on the lounge chair in the sunroom and dreamed of Donovan. When she awoke, it was close to 5:30 p.m. Jade showered, changed, and headed to Donovan's house to help with dinner. She was sure that her mom was there already.

On the walk to Donovan's house, his words echoed in her ears. "Until you want me...I will continue to love you. I'll see you this evening." What! What did he mean? He wasn't scheduled to return from North Carolina for three more days. Jade quickened her pace to the house. She needed to confirm Donovan's return with Ms. Evelyn.

Jade entered Donovan's home through the back door, totally unprepared for the scene that played out before her. Her mom, Ms. Evelyn, the twins, Donovan's mother, his sister, and one teenage girl were preparing dinner. It looked like a Sunday feast for 30, but it was a Thursday. Jade noticed the cabbage, greens, green beans seasoned with onions, cream corn, sweet cornbread, fried chicken, and she smelled other mouth-watering aromas. What was going on?

Overwhelmed by the implications and glad that no one had heard her entrance, Jade turned to leave. Then she felt a soft hand intertwine with hers and looked down into the face of Kamia. Although she was not Donovan's biological daughter, she was a perfect reflection of him.

"Jade, where are you going?"

"Hey, Kamia. Sweetie, I, well..."

"Oh my goodness, Jade!" Danielle, Donovan's sister, greeted her with a hug. "You look amazing. Sydnee, come here. This is Jade. Jade, this is Sydnee, Gavin's daughter. Do you remember Gavin, Donovan's friend?"

"Nice to meet you, Ms. Jade. My Uncle's really into you.

Oops, sorry," Sydnee said, covering her mouth with both hands.

"Don't be sorry; I am sure Jade is aware that Donovan digs her," Danielle replied.

Sharron, Donovan's mother, moved closer to Jade and greeted her with a smile.

"Hello, dear. You didn't think I would let Ms. Evelyn have you all to herself, did you? You look angelic. I am so sorry, sweetheart…for your pain…but I am thankful for you being in our lives again," she said as she embraced Jade.

The tears that were pooling in Jade's eyes spilled over and wouldn't stop. Sharron's arms tightened around her and then Jade felt additional arms embrace her. They were arms of wisdom, arms of youthfulness, and arms of innocence, but all were arms of love. Jade continued to cry, for she knew that this moment would change her forever.

The door swung open and in strolled two handsome men. All the women turned at the sound. Jade recognized one man as Gavin, Donovan's best friend, and the other as Daniel, Donovan's father. Donovan was not among them. The men gazed the room to assess the situation.

"Sharron, what's going on?" asked Daniel.

"Honey, we're fine," Sharron replied.

Donovan entered the house behind the two men with luggage in both hands. His face reflected sheer exhaustion as he looked around the room. The click and clatter ceased when the deadening sound of Donovan's voice asked, "What's going on? Jade, are you okay?"

He dropped the luggage and approached the women, who were still embracing with tears on their faces.

Sharron spoke calmly, "Donovan, honey, we're fine; this is women's business. Men, please leave the kitchen, go wash up, and prepare for dinner. We've prepared all your favorites."

Jade noticed that the other men waited for Donovan to respond.

Donovan's eyes focused on Jade, and she nodded to

reassure him that she was all right. He looked to her mom and then to his mom. In one swift motion, he turned around, retrieved the luggage, and headed up the stairs.

"Girls, go upstairs and wash up for dinner," Sharron instructed.

Kamia and Kamill looked up at Jade with worry etched on their faces.

"I am fine. Please go upstairs and check on your dad. Tell him all about the fun things we've done this week," Jade said while wiping the remaining tears from her face.

"Donovan has been unbearable this week. Of all the years that I've known him, Donovan has never seemed so preoccupied and unsure of himself," Gavin said.

Daniel turned toward Jade and said, "Honestly, I don't remember the details of your past relationship with my son. But it is clear to me that he can't fathom his future without you. He feels vulnerable, which generates fear. And fear for Donovan generates anger. Fear and anger will cause his heart to harden. I love my son and my son loves you. Sometimes you have to take a chance on love. There is comfort in knowing that true love never ceases. It remains in the heart. It can move aside and makes room for other loves, but it never ceases."

"Well, you all have given Jade a lot to think about. Perhaps she and Donovan should have dinner alone tonight and talk," Pearl said.

"Yes, of course," Sharron replied.

"Jade, how do you feel about that? I don't want you to feel any added pressure," her mom asked.

Jade thought, Wow! Are they serious?

"Thank you all for your concern. But, please excuse me," Jade said on her way out of the back door.

Jade texted Donovan, "Please meet me at Tia's house in twenty minutes. We need to talk," Jade said, before walking out of the door.

Then she called Tia. "Tia, Donovan's entire family is here. It's like a mini-family reunion. I don't know what to think, but it feels overwhelming with the 'welcome back to the family' comments." She paused. "Tia, why haven't you said anything? What are you doing?" Jade asked.

"Jade, I'm on a date," Tia whispered.

"You're on a date. Oh my. I'm so sorry. Why would you answer the phone? Is it a good date?

"Yes."

"Yes. Well, apologize for answering the phone. Explain to him that I've been sick. Then turn off your phone. Love ya! Bye. "

Jade attempted to call Onyx, but the call went straight to voicemail.

"Great, just great!"

Jade paced back and forth wondering what to say to Donovan.

Chapter Eight

When Jade opened the door, Donovan sensed her anxiety. But the only thing on his mind was satisfying his need to kiss her. She looked stunning in a light green sleeveless wrap dress with cream sandals. He was very much aware of her generous cleavage, curvy hips, and sexy legs. His eyes then moved upward and zeroed in on her face, which was more beautiful than ever.

Jade opened the door and marveled at how handsome Donovan looked. He was dressed in a butter cream linen suit, leather sandals the color of peanut butter, and his thin yellow gold Figaro chain necklace with a K charm.

Jade hadn't realized that she was holding her breath until Donovan reached for her hand. The connecting of their hands sent small molecules of electricity throughout her body. Jade stepped closer to Donovan, molding her body to him

"Donovan" was the only word that escaped Jade's lips before his mouth covered hers. Jade swayed and felt like her legs were turning to jelly. Donovan wrapped his arm around her waist and pulled her close. He captured her tongue and made love to her mouth, evoking memories she'd tried to suppress over the years. He withdrew his tongue only to trace the outline of her lips, and then he placed featherlike kisses on the corners of her mouth as he whispered against her lips. "Sweetheart, I am starving for more than food. So we should probably leave. Are you ready?"

"Yes," was all Jade could manage to say. She had no idea what to do with her emotional connection and physical attraction to Donovan. She hoped by the end of the night that she would have a better perspective on everything.

Donovan and Jade shared a delicious meal at Skippers' Fish Camp in Darien, Georgia. The atmosphere of the restaurant allowed for easy conversation. Although they were aware that they needed to talk about what was going on between them, neither knew how to approach the subject.

Jade wondered if things could really work between them, in spite of the issues in their past relationship. Everyone experienced regrets and questioned past decisions. Fourteen years ago, they were different people, and in different spaces in their lives, but they had experienced love together. People change, as she had, but was their love worth exploring? They needed to talk about their past relationship and the effect it had on her life.

"Donovan, before we can talk about what is happening between us now, we need to talk about what happened between us in the past. What do you remember about our relationship?"

"I remember that you consumed my whole world and nothing else really mattered to me. I loved you with all my heart, but you ended our relationship and walked away. The hurt was overwhelming; it was like nothing I had ever experienced before. My love for you was on the purest level. So, if your happiness was not with me, then that's the price I had to pay. It took time and effort for me to heal. When I met Asia, she accepted me with all of my flaws. She was patient with me as I learned to trust again."

Donovan took a deep breath and said, "Now tell me what you remember about our relationship."

Through the steady stream of tears falling from her eyes, Jade found the courage to look at Donovan and said, "I remember that I loved you on purpose with no thought about the consequences. I loved you unconditionally. Every time I saw you or heard your voice, my heart would literally skip a beat, anticipating what was to come. When you said my name... whether I was sitting across from you eating, walking with you, or making love with you, my spirit smiled at the reflection of love in your eyes and your voice. I loved you so much that each time I looked in the mirror I saw more of your reflection than my own. I was afraid that Jade would be totally consumed by Donovan and cease to exist. I ended our relationship to preserve me.

"Afterward, my heart was broken and I did not want to trust in love again. Then I met Jonothan. He loved me as I was. He helped me learn to trust and believe in love again. I learned that I could love someone totally without losing sight of myself."

"Jade, the love we shared was amazing, but God makes no mistakes; His timing is perfect." Donovan reached for Jade's hand across the table. "It would be a privilege to love you again."

Jade took a deep breath before she continued to speak. "My love for you never wavered. It remained hidden in the smallest corner of my heart. I kept the memories of our love hidden in the deepest creases of my mind. The memories would surface with a familiar melody or the aroma of certain foods, and at the oddest times in my life. I used to dream of a beautiful little girl with milk chocolate skin, your full face, big vibrant cinnamon-colored eyes, your nose, my smile, and thick little legs…named Diamond. Donovan, there is so much more that I need to tell you."

It was at that moment that Jade realized that she had been grieving for more than Jonothan and Amber. Her grief was complicated and rooted deeply in years of unresolved feelings. She grieved the loss of what she and Donovan's love had meant to her life and the loss of what their love could have been.

During the drive back to the island, Kem's voice echoed throughout the car. His melody "Share My Life" soothed Jade's emotions. The song was interrupted by simultaneous rings of Donovan's and Jade's cell phones. As Donovan answered his phone, Jade's phone stopped ringing.

From the sheer panic that appeared on Donovan's face, Jade knew that something was wrong. As soon as he disconnected the call, he told her what it was about.

"Kamill has the gift of dreams. Her dreams are inspirational revelations or warnings of danger to anyone that she connects with emotionally. She started having them about three years ago. I was on a flight back from Kuwait and the plane had difficulty with the landing gear, which led to a minor crash. Kamill, Kamia, Ms. Evelyn, and my parents were at the airport waiting for me. I hadn't told anyone that I was flying in that morning, but they were all there. Ms. Evelyn said Kamill dreamt the plane crashed. As a result of that incident, I purchased a private plane and contracted with three pilots for all future plane trips.

"It was her dream that led us to you that morning on the beach. So please understand that we take her dreams seriously. Kamill just had a dream about her biological sister and brother. The twins know that they are adopted, but I've never told them about their sister and brother. Mom said that Kamia and Kamill are waiting to talk to me. Jade, I don't know if I'm ready for this conversation."

"Donovan, you are a wonderful father; the words will come," Jade responded.

"Jade, after I talk with the girls, I'm flying back to Atlanta tonight. Will you go with me? I know that it's a lot to ask, but I need you."

"Yes, I'll go with you. Donovan, everything will be fine," Jade said as she caressed his hand.

She intertwined her fingers with Donovan's. She silently prayed for Kamia, Kamill, their siblings, and Donovan.

When Donovan opened the door to the house, he greeted Ms. Evelyn.

Ms. Evelyn stood, reached for his hand, and said, "Your mom and the girls are lying down in their room."

"Thank you," Donovan said as he walked toward the girl's room.

When Donovan walked into the room, there were four innocent eyes full of fear looking up at him. His mother excused herself from the room.

He sat down on the bed and Kamill said, "Daddy, there's something wrong. I had a sad dream."

"Come here, baby. Can you tell me about the dream?"

"I dreamed of a girl and a boy standing next to a bed holding a man's hand. They were crying. When the girl looked up at me, she had the same face as mine and Kamia's. Then when the boy looked up, his face was different, but I felt like I knew them both. Daddy, I don't understand," Kamia said quietly.

"Kamill and Kamia, remember when Daddy talked with you about being adopted?"

"Yes," they answered in unison.

"Well, Daddy didn't explain everything. You have a sister. Her name is Natalie and she is fourteen. You have a brother too, and his name is Khalil and he is fifteen. They live with their dad, Nathan," he explained.

"Daddy, what if something happens to their dad? Who will take care of them?" Kamia asked.

Donovan thought of Kamia's question and its implications.

"Daddy, do you know where my sister and my brother live?" Kamia asked.

"Yes, I do."

"Daddy, will you go check on them?" Kamill pleaded.

Donovan sighed and shook his head, thinking that his selfless eight-year-old daughters were precious and innocent. In their minds, it was that simple: their father was supposed to be able to go help and fix everything.

"Are you sure that's okay with you?" he asked.

"Yes, please go and make sure they're okay," Kamill answered.

"I will."

"Daddy, will you say prayers with us before you leave?" Kamia asked.

Donovan prayed with his children, tucked them in, and kissed them good night. Donovan went to his room. He searched his phone for Nathan's cell number.

"You've reached Nathan…"

"Nathan, it's Donovan, call me back when you get this message."

When Donovan called Nathan's house number, the answering machine picked up. He left a voice message. Donovan became worried when Nathan didn't return his call or respond by text. Donovan pulled out his small luggage and packed a few things. He sat on the bed and placed his face in his hands, then rubbed his temples. He reached for his cell phone again, he dialed Nathan's number, "Man, call me back. I'm worried about you and the kids."

Donovan retrieved his luggage and returned to the family room. He explained to his family that his attempts to reach Nathan by phone were unsuccessfully and that he was leaving for Atlanta that evening.

"Where is Jade?" Donovan asked.

"She went to Tia's house to pack," Ms. Evelyn said.

Chapter Nine

J ade and Donovan arrived at McKinnon Airport in record time. To Jade's amazement, there was a small private plane with the initial K on it. Once safely in the air, Donovan made several more calls to Nathan and his fiancée, Ameilia, but was unable to reach them. He squeezed Jade's hand and spoke, in a shaking voice, "Something is very wrong. I can feel it in the pit of my stomach."

Donovan explained how our families were connected. Natalie and Khalil are half-siblings of Kamia and Kamill. The children's biological mother, Kyla, married her high school sweetheart, Nathan. They divorced, but maintained a respectful co-parenting relationship. Then Kyla got pregnant with Kamill and Kamia from another relationship. She passed away due to complications during delivery and the twins' biological father's identity was unknown. Kyla's mother, Ms. Kora, was given custody of the four children. When Ms. Kora was diagnosed with an early onset of Alzheimer's disease, she contacted Nathan and he assumed full custody of his children. Ms. Kora decided to find an adoptive family for the twins.

Ms. Kora was Asia's secretary. She knew how desperately Donovan and his wife wanted children and approached them about adopting the twins. After Asia's death, Ms. Kora asked Donovan to still consider adopting the girls, but with stipulations. She asked him to become her power of attorney, bring the twins to visit her once a week, and reunite the twins with their siblings by their tenth birthday. He insisted that Ms. Kora move in with them, but she preferred to move to Peachtree Manor, an upscale nursing facility in Fayetteville, Georgia. After he agreed to her stipulations, she introduced him to Nathan."

Donovan took a deep breath and looked into Jade's eyes, but before he could speak she said, "Don't you dare apologize."

He chuckled and said, "You could always read my thoughts and complete my sentences. Let's face it, this is a lot."

"You are not hard to read, Mr. Johnson. Now tell me about Nathan."

"Nathan was a skilled construction worker. His woodwork was phenomenal. He was working odd jobs when we met. I was so impressed by his craft and skill with wood that I called in a favor from a friend at Dorsey Construction and they hired Nathan as a full-time foreman. This job provided him with benefits and better working hours.

"Over the years, we've become good friends. We had to coordinate our schedules to ensure that our visitation with Ms. Kora didn't overlap. We would have lunch once a month to talk about Ms. Kora, the kids, and share pictures. We stopped having lunch together months ago because of conflicted schedules. I didn't think, I just didn't know."

"Have you met Natalie and Khalil?" Jade asked curiously.

"I met them both four years ago during Christmas. Natalie was 10 and Khalil was 11. Khalil thanked me for adopting and taking care of his siblings. I showed them the twins' pictures. Nathan and I explained to them that we would reunite them when the twins turned 10 years old. I could tell that they didn't agree with our plans, but accepted it. I've attended several of Natalie's and Khalil's basketball games and track meets during the past two years. Natalie and Khalil are both very mature for their ages. Now Natalie is fourteen and Khalil is fifteen."

"Donovan, it sounds like these children have experienced a lot of loss and challenging circumstances," Jade said, wiping a tear from her eye.

"They have. It's funny how we have a plan and God has a different plan."

Donovan's comment was interrupted by an incoming call from Amelia, Nathan's fiancée.

"Amelia, is everything okay with Nathan and the children?" he asked.

"No, Donovan."

There was a long pause before Amelia resumed speaking.

"Nathan passed away today around 2 p.m. at the Beverly Ann Grace Hospice Center. He had prostate cancer. Where are you?" Amelia asked.

"Passed away...cancer." Donovan couldn't believe what Amelia had just said. "I'm flying back to Atlanta. Amelia, where are Natalie and Khalil?"

Amelia informed Donovan that Nathan had appointed him as the legal guardian of Natalie and Khalil. Social Services would not grant Amelia temporary guardianship of the children until Donovan was located and notified. The children were placed together in a temporary foster home.

"Donovan, I need a day or so just to process everything. But please call me if the children need me," Amelia said, through her sobs.

"I will. Thank you for calling me," Donovan replied.

Donovan explained everything to Jade, shortly before they landed at Hartsfield-Jackson Atlanta International Airport he contacted the on-call Social Services Supervisor to arrange to pick up the children. Jade texted her mom, Onyx, and Tia to let them know that they had arrived safely.

"Donovan, it's midnight; maybe we should let the children sleep until the morning."

"No! Nathan just died. They have no familiar faces to share their grief with. They'll need me. We are picking them up within the hour."

"Okay. Why don't we go to your house in College Park first? It's the closest, right? A long drive isn't good for us right now. It may aggravate the situation." When Donovan nodded, she asked, "Is the house stocked with clean linens and food?"

"How did you know that I still owned that house?" Donovan asked with a questioning look.

"That's your family's home. You would never sell the house or even rent it out. It means too much to you."

Chapter Ten

Donovan and Jade arrived at the foster parents' home and were greeted by friendly faces. He thanked the family for understanding his concern for the children and for all they had done.

Both children looked exhausted and emotionally drained.

"Uncle D, my dad said that you would come," Khalil said with a partial smile. He was a handsome young man. His complexion was deep chocolate, with the same hazel eyes as the twins. He was also tall, at least 6 feet. His hair was cut in a close-cropped fade. Jade assumed that his features and complexion were those of his father, because they were different from his sister's.

Natalie's skin was the color of caramel and her eyes were hazel. She was tall, standing at 5'8" and her hair was in Senegalese braids. Her features made her look like an older version of Kamill and Kamia. Jade assumed that the girls' features were those of their biological mother.

She started to cry. "Uncle Donovan, my daddy died today." She held onto Donovan and Khalil for physical support. The scene was heartbreaking.

The car ride was silent, with the exception of Donovan's radio quietly playing Coltrane in the background. No words needed to be spoken. Natalie fell asleep. Khalil was awake, listening to music on his phone. Jade sat silently and prayed for the children, for Donovan, and herself.

When they arrived at Donovan's childhood home, several lights were on. Jade looked to Donovan for an explanation. "I called a friend to stock the house with food and put clean linen on the beds."

Donovan gave Jade the key to the house. The place smelled of cinnamon and vanilla, two of Jade's favorite scents. She believed in the calming effect of aromatherapy.

She maneuvered through the house with ease. Warmth

permeated throughout the house, and Jade was pleased with their decision to bring the children there.

Khalil and Donovan guided a very sleepy Natalie into the house and to the master bedroom. Once she was on the bed, Khalil removed Natalie's earrings, shoes, and socks. He covered her up and kissed her cheek. He placed her earrings on the side table. "She is an angel who sleeps like a log and snores like a bear," he chuckled.

Jade's eyes filled with tears as she processed Khalil's sincere concern for his sister. He too had experienced loss, but his priority was Natalie.

"She's lucky to have you as a brother. Let me show you where the bathroom and your room are."

Khalil said, "If that is okay. I'll sleep in here with Natalie."

Donovan spoke. "Of course that's okay."

*****

Donovan woke to the smell of coffee and a delicious breakfast. He looked towards the bed and saw Khalil at its foot, asleep. He and Jade didn't want to leave the children alone, so they'd slept in the recliners in the room. He heard Jade and Natalie talking and stirring around in the house. He showered, changed, and prayed for strength for the journey set before him.

Donovan walked into the kitchen and found Jade sipping a cup of coffee.

"Good morning. What have you two been up to?"

"What do you mean?" Jade smiled and looked at Natalie.

Natalie was standing at the stove stirring a pot of grits.

When I got up Natalie was up cooking. Doesn't it smell delightful?

She gestured for him to have a seat. She fixed Donovan a cup of coffee with cream and sugar. As she was placing the coffee on the table, Natalie gave him a plate loaded with grits, eggs, salmon croquets, and homemade biscuits topped with honey and butter.

"Natalie, sit and eat. I will go check on Khalil," Jade said.

To her surprise, Khalil was up and dressed.

"Good morning, Khalil. Natalie made breakfast."

"She loves to cook. I'm glad she's good at it."

"Let's get you something to eat." They walked into the kitchen.

"Good morning," Khalil said, looking between Natalie and Donovan.

"Have a seat and I'll fix your plate," Jade insisted.

"After you eat, we'll discuss everything and follow your lead," Donovan said to Natalie and Khalil.

He turned to Jade and she nodded in approval. She knew the impact that a sudden death and grief could have on a person.

Natalie and Khalil looked up with relief in their eyes. They were thankful that Donovan would allow them to be involved and make some of the decisions themselves.

After everyone finished eating breakfast, Natalie and Khalil told them that their dad was diagnosed with prostate cancer seven months ago.

Donovan wished that he had been a support for Nathan and the children during that time.

Khalil must have sensed Donovan's feelings of guilt.

"Uncle D, my dad didn't want you or Grandma Kora to know that he was sick. I don't know why, but he didn't. While he was sick, we had help from Amelia and the staff at Beverly Ann Grace Hospice."

"The hospice social workers told us what to expect. But yesterday, none of that mattered." Natalie put her head down to hide her tears. "He passed away with us holding his hand."

Khalil touched his sister's shoulder before speaking, "Dad wanted us to be prepared. Dad told me that all his important documents were in his safe. He helped me memorize the combination. He asked us what was most important to us and we told him the twins and Grandma Kora."

Donovan and Khalil talked about going to Nathan's home

to pick up the documents.

"Natalie, would you like to go with us to the house?" Donovan asked.

"No," Natalie said as she excused herself from the table. She went to the sink and started rinsing the dishes to place them in the dishwasher.

Jade joined her. "I'll go with you if you would like," she offered.

"No, thanks. I'm not ready to go back there now. Khalil, will you pack up everything that I'll need until..." Natalie's sentence trailed off into silence.

"Okay. That's fine. Why don't you go lie down and I'll finish the dishes later?" Jade said, ushering Natalie out of the kitchen.

Later that morning, Donovan and Khalil arrived at Nathan's home in Marietta, GA. Donovan was careful not to disturb anything in the house. When Khalil handed him the legal documents and letters from the safe, he excused himself to pack more clothes and personal items for himself and Natalie.

As Donovan glanced through the letters, he found that they were addressed to the children, Amelia, Joshua (Nathan's brother), and himself. Then he found another envelope addressed to him that read, "OPEN BEFORE YOU LEAVE THE HOUSE."

Donovan,

Please give the letters to the kids, Amelia, and Joshua after the service. Read your letter and the other information as soon as you can.

Nathan

During the drive back to the house, Donovan prayed for guidance and gave thanks for his life and his family. He also prayed and gave thanks for Natalie, Khalil, and Jade.

He called Jade from his cell phone to tell her how much he appreciated her.

"Hey, you," Donovan said upon hearing Jade's voice.

"Hi," Jade answered.

"How are you?" Donovan asked.

"I'm fine. I'm worried about you. You only had three hours of sleep," Jade said with concern.

"Babe, I'm good. Thank you for being here with me."

"You're welcome," Jade replied.

"You're pretty amazing. How is Natalie?"

"She's okay. She's taking nap," Jade answered.

Donovan looked over at Khalil in the passenger seat. "Khalil is too. We'll be there in twenty minutes," Donovan answered.

"Okay. Maybe we'll all rest better tonight." Jade knew the answer to that comment, but she continued. "Are we staying here another night or are we going back to St. Simons?"

"We're going to my home in Fayetteville. Traffic will be light for the next hour or so. Will you pack everything up?"

"I've packed most of it. How long will it take to get to your house from here?"

"Forty-five minutes to an hour. That's only if we leave soon after I return. Khalil and I have already eaten lunch; would you like me to pick something up for you and Natalie?"

"No, we've already eaten. Drive safely," Jade replied.

*****

They were not able to leave Donovan's childhood home in a reasonable time to avoid traffic. Instead, they all took an hour and a half nap before leaving, but Jade, Natalie, and Khalil still fell asleep during the ride.

Donovan looked over at Jade as she stirred and opened her eyes. He was pulling up the circular driveway to the house.

"Donovan, this is a mansion, not a house!" she said.

Natalie and Khalil woke up and their jaws dropped open at the sight.

Donovan gave them a tour of the main house. He mentioned that he also had a guest house and told them they had more than enough time to go there later. The house had three levels, including the basement. The main level consisted of a massive foyer, the family room, the formal dining room, formal sitting room, kitchen with a dining area, a laundry room, a guest room with a bathroom, a master bedroom with a bathroom, a half bath, and Donovan's home office. There was a winding staircase that led to the upper level where four more bedrooms with adjoining bathrooms were located. The twins also had their own playroom. In the basement were the gym and another guest room. The grounds included a deck with an outdoor kitchen, garden, pool, and a basketball court.

During the tour, Donovan pointed out room options for Natalie and Khalil. Natalie chose the guest room upstairs and Khalil selected the one in the basement.

Around 6 p.m., Jade and Natalie entered the kitchen. Natalie wanted to prepare dinner for the four of them.

"Wow! This is an amazing kitchen. I'm afraid to touch anything," Natalie said.

"Don't be silly. I'm sure Ms. Evelyn will not mind you cooking in her kitchen," Jade responded.

"Exactly, *her* kitchen. I feel like I am trespassing. Who is Ms. Evelyn? Is she the cook? Maybe we should call and ask her first."

"No, she is not the cook. She helps Donovan with the girls and manages the house."

"Oh, like a nanny."

"Sort of, now come on. I think that's the pantry. Let's check it out. We may have to go grocery shopping."

Jade was just about to ask Natalie what she wanted to cook, but both stood in awe at the contents in the pantry. It was well organized and stocked with a large variety of food. All of the kitchen appliances were neatly stored on the wall opposite the food. There were two freezers lined up on the back wall. One freezer was stocked with meats and the otherwith frozen vegetables. The pots were stored on a pot rack that was anchored to the ceiling.

"How many people does she cook for and how does she reach those pots? Man, this is too much. I've never seen anything like this," Natalie stated.

"Neither have I." Jade chuckled and looked around on the walls. "There is probably a button that suspends the rack."

"Ms. Jade, I think we should call Ms. Evelyn."

"Call me Jade. And you win; we'll call her."

Jade dialed Ms. Evelyn's number. "Ms. Evelyn, hi. Yes, ma'am, we're fine. We just arrived to the main house. Natalie and I don't feel comfortable using the kitchen without your permission," she said sheepishly.

"Jade, honey," Ms. Evelyn said, "I am not territorial. Make yourself at home. For the record, it is Natalie's home now. The button for the pot rack is on the wall next to the light. If there is something you want to eat that is not in the house, call Sam's Grocery. The number is on the inside cover of the cookbook on the counter. They deliver."

"Thank you."

"You're welcome, and don't forget that Donovan is allergic to pineapple. Jade, I need to ask you something, please walk outside of the room," Ms. Evelyn requested.

"Yes, ma'am," Jade said before whispering, "I'll be back," to Natalie.

Jade went outside on the deck so that she could speak in private.

"Okay, we can speak in private now. I'm on the deck," Jade said.

"That's one of my favorite outside spots. Jade, how are Natalie and Khalil doing? What can we do?"

"They are okay, under the circumstances. I was hoping Natalie would take it easy today, but she insists on cooking. I think it's her coping mechanism."

"Jade, they can claim any available space in the house. I've been thinking of possible renovations and additions that may be needed."

"Ms. Evelyn, this house is huge; what possible renovations or additions will be needed?"

"Any changes that will accommodate our growing family, or make the house a home for Natalie and Khalil. Donovan is not going to offer any input on this, so I will ask for your input from time to time."

Jade felt uneasy by Ms. Evelyn's comment. Why would she want Jade's input on the renovations for Donovan's house? When Jade returned to the kitchen she hid her true feeling inside.

"Natalie, Ms. Evelyn said the kitchen is all yours."

Natalie was thrilled to have full access and control of the kitchen. Jade assisted her in preparing dinner and dessert. After dinner, Natalie and Khalil settled into their rooms and went to sleep early.

Donovan and Jade stayed up late that night going through the packets of information that Nathan had put together. Nathan prepaid and pre-arranged his funeral services in detail, including an outline of the program. His last will and testament named Donovan as the legal guardian for Natalie and Khalil. Nathan left a substantial monetary gift to his fiancée, Amelia. He left his childhood home in Marietta to Natalie and Khalil. Nathan arranged for the property to become an income property for both children. He instructed Donovan to contact *Henry Lee Chambers's Realty*. His car was to be placed in storage until Natalie turned sixteen in two years. Nathan's note said, "I want to give my baby girl her first car."

Donovan was impressed and grateful that Nathan had been so thorough in his preparation for his children. Nathan knew that Donovan would love the children and could provide for them financially, but he wanted to leave them a legacy. He had followed Donovan's recommendations for investments, and they more than secured his children's financial futures. He had also established a trust fund that would release funds on each of the children's eighteenth and thirtieth birthdays.

The last packet contained the kids' medical information: copies of their immunizations, recent physicals, the names and phone numbers of their doctors, a list of their current medications, and a list of their allergies.

"Nathan left letters for me, the children, Amelia, and Joshua," Donovan showed Jade the letters.

"Who is Joshua?"

"Joshua is Nathan's fraternal twin brother. He is a member of the United States Army Elite Special Forces. If he's away on a mission, even if we contact the American Red Cross for assistance with notification, he may not be reachable at this point."

"Really, are you serious?"

"Yeah, but I hope that's not the case.

Jade noticed that Donovan was visibly shaken by the envelope in his hands. She kissed him softly on the lips and excused herself from the room, giving him time alone.

Donovan's heart clenched at the envelope attached to the last packet of information. The letter read:

Donovan,

You have been a great friend and I say with much pride that it was a privilege to know that you will raise my children in my absence. Kyla would have wanted her children to be together and near Ms. Kora. I know that you will be a great father to Khalil and Natalie.

Thank you for helping me get my career on track and for the advice you gave that has secured my children's financial future. Please forgive me for not telling you about the cancer. I didn't tell you because you would have wanted to fix it. I just wanted to spend my last few months spending time with my children and Amelia.

Amelia is very attached to the children and may have a difficult time accepting that the children are with you. But, Amelia is young and beautiful, love will find its way to her again. She needs to be free and open to it when it comes.

Joshua was away on a mission when I was initially diagnosed. So, he won't know of my illness and possibly my death until his return. He will understand my decision to give you custody of the children. He has a successful career that would not allow him to raise two teenagers.

Now, let me tell you about the wonderful children that you've inherited. Khalil is an intelligent, strong, and responsible young man. He has a true gift for making connections with other people. He is popular in school and motivated to excel in his academics. He is athletic and loves basketball and football. He is not on any medication and has no known food allergies. He will try to father Natalie, but make sure he doesn't. They are very close, only 16 months apart. He tends to fall hard for girls. He and Mia have been dating for a while now. He has been educated on safe sex, and to my knowledge, they have not had sex. His best friend is Delshon. Khalil plans to attend Georgia Tech when he graduates from high school. His aspiration is to become an engineer. Yes, you will have to wear the yellow and gold to show support.

Natalie is simply precious, like a beautiful butterfly. My baby girl views life's opportunities as limitless. She grows and adapts well to most situations. She is still searching for the Natalie she is most comfortable with. She is adventurous and courageous, and she, too, is very athletic. She loves basketball, track, and softball. She is very intelligent and excels in school. Although popular, she is somewhat reserved. Her best friend is Lyric. Their friendship is very important to Natalie. Natalie is allergic to kiwi. She suffers from asthma and uses an inhaler. She plans to attend Spelman College and would like to major in Business Management. She loves to cook and plans to attend Culinary School and open a restaurant after she graduates from Spelman. You will have to exercise to keep the weight off, because she is an awesome cook. Compiling a cookbook of her family recipes is important to her. Beware of the BOYS. They are looking. Natalie will need help with relationships, because she doesn't trust easily.

Ms. Kora and I left a log of our family history information. Please make sure the children learn all about their family. It's a part of them and now it's a part of you.

You have to be the one to tell Ms. Kora that I've passed away. By the way, you need a woman who can love you and be a great mother to all four of your children. Go get Jade--you told me about her, not much, but enough for me to know that you still love her.

Donovan, they are wonderful children. Love them. Protect them. Give them wonderful memories to carry in their hearts.

One last thing: please tell my children daily that I love them.

May the blessings of God reign in your life, the lives of our children, and of all those you love.

I am eternally grateful to you,

Nathan

Donovan's tears added to the already tear stained letter. He felt honored that Nathan entrusted the care of his children to him. He always wanted a house full of children, but he didn't know God's plan would lead him on this journey.

Reading the letter had been too overwhelming. Donovan sought out Jade as his source of comfort.

"Hi. I just finished reading Nathan's letter," Donovan said, entering the laundry room where Jade was ironing Natalie's and Khalil's clothes. He leaned against the wall for support.

Jade looked up into his eyes and moved towards him. How could the connection between them be so strong, so soon?

"Is there anything I can do?

"I'll call everyone in the morning to give them an update. I have to call the base where Joshua is stationed. Then I'll talk with Natalie and Khalil about the family coming into town to attend the funeral. It may be too overwhelming for the children if everyone flew in at once. There are several loose ends that we need take care of. I need to go tell Ms. Kora. Will you go with me?"

"Shhh. Of course I will," she said. She would do just about anything he asked.

"I know it's a lot to ask, but I….."

He reached for her and pulled her close. He held on to Jade, more for himself than for her. Donovan felt safe in her arms and allowed himself to cry.

Jade didn't say a word, but in her heart she prayed for him as she held up Donovan's frame against her.

"I'm sorry," he whispered against her neck.

"Shhh, don't be. Only strong men allow themselves to cry. And you, Donovan Johnson are a *strong man*."

Chapter Eleven

The next morning, everyone slept late. Natalie was the last to wake up at noon. After lunch, Donovan talked with Natalie and Khalil about the funeral arrangements that Nathan made.

"I've called the Army Base where your Uncle Joshua is stationed. Unfortunately, I haven't heard back from anyone.

"I want you to know that you are now a part of my family. You will have the opportunity to meet my parents, Daniel and Sharron Johnson, and my sister Danielle. She and I are very close, like the two of you. Ms. Evelyn, well, she lives with me and helps me care for the twins. She is like a second mom to me, and the twins call her Granny. She has been a part of our family for four years. Gavin is my best friend. We have been best friends since third grade. He is like a brother to me, and the twins call him uncle. Gavin has a daughter Sydnee, who is fifteen. All of these people are important to me and will be a part of your life. I know that it will take some time getting used to all of us, but we will take it one day at a time.

"My family would like to attend the service and be here to support you. Allowing them to attend or not will be your decision. Think about it and let me know.

"Now I want you to tell me about your family and the friends that are important to you," Donovan continued.

"Uncle Joshua, my dad's twin brother, Grandma Kora, Amelia, and the twins are our only family," Khalil said. "We haven't seen or heard from Uncle Joshua since Thanksgiving. And, well, we haven't seen the twins since they were three years old.

"My best friend's name is Delshon. We've been friends since we were twelve. My girlfriend's name is Mia. We've been dating for two years. I would like for them to come to the service." Khalil looked at Natalie, prompting her to speak next.

"My best friend's name is Lyric and well...I don't have a

boyfriend," she said. "I would like for Lyric to come to the service, too."

Unconsciously, Donovan released the breath he was holding. Boyfriends and girlfriends! Too much!

"Of course your friends can attend the service," Jade said. "We'll call their parents and make arrangements for transportation."

"Thank you," the children said.

"When will Kamill and Kamia get here?" Natalie asked, her voice strained with anxiety.

Donovan was saddened by the pain in Natalie's and Khalil's eyes. He reached out and put his hands on top of both of theirs. "Well, I would like for us to get some things taken care of before the girls come back. Hopefully, they'll be here in a couple of days."

Khalil withdrew his hand and asked, "Will you take us to see Grandma Kora today?"

"Yes, I will. I need to tell her about your father. We'll stay as long as you would like."

"We've talked about our family and friends; now, Ms. Jade, tell us who you are," Natalie said.

Jade and Donovan looked at each other, searching for something to say.

Khalil asked, "Are you two dating or engaged?"

"They're not engaged. She's not wearing a ring," Natalie stated.

Jade looked sternly at Donovan and said, "We are friends."

"Friends? Ms. Jade...friends?" Natalie asked.

"Look, please call me Jade, not Ms. Jade."

"Okay. Do you have family?"

"Yes, my mom's name is Pearl and she is actually in St. Simons with Donovan's family and the girls right now. My sister's name is Onyx."

"Friends," Khalil repeated in a sarcastic tone.

"Are we going to meet Onyx when the rest of the family comes?" Natalie asked.

"No, Onyx lives in Hawaii," Jade replied.

Natalie looked at Donovan and said, "I want your family to come."

Donovan looked at Khalil, who was preoccupied with his cell phone. He turned towards Natalie before answering.

"Okay."

*****

That evening, Natalie, Jade, Khalil, and Donovan went to visit Ms. Kora at Peachtree Manor. Donovan stopped by the nurse's station to speak with the floor nurse.

"Hello, Mr. Johnson."

"Hello, Shonda."

"Hello, Natalie, Khalil, and …I apologize, but I don't believe we've met," the nurse said to Jade.

"I'm Jade." Jade offered no further explanation.

"Shonda, how was Kora's day?" Donovan asked.

"Kora was sad today. She said that someone very special to her died yesterday. She has had several restless nights. Her dreams are back."

"Shonda, Nathan died yesterday. We came to tell her."

"Oh, my God, her dreams," Shonda said, covering her mouth.

Jade instinctively covered her mouth, also. She wondered if Ms. Kora also had a gift of dreams like Kamill did.

"She asked to be put in bed early last night and again tonight."

Donovan led the way to Ms. Kora's room, which was dimly lit. Before Donovan could call her name, Ms. Kora's eyes opened. Although she suffered from dementia, she recognized her grandchildren and Donovan, who she called "Donnie."

Ms. Kora adjusted the head of the bed until she was in an upright position. "Come children, Natalie and Khalil, sit."

The children immediately moved to Ms. Kora's bedside.

"Donnie, you come closer. Nathan left us. I saw Nathan

and Kyla walking, talking, and holding hands in heaven. They always loved each other, but sometimes the circumstances of life overshadows love and clouds our vision." She reached for Natalie and Khalil's hands. "Now children, I know that you are sad. So am I, and your Uncle D is too, but we are still living. Most of your family is right here in this room. Donnie will take care of us. Won't you, Donnie?"

"Yes, ma'am," Donovan responded through his own tears.

"Donnie, where are the twins, and who is that young lady?" she asked.

"Ms. Kora, the girls are at the beach. This is my friend Jade." Donovan laughed in spite of the situation, thinking the doctor needed to re-evaluate Ms. Kora's dementia diagnosis.

After spending thirty minutes talking, a knock at the door interrupted Ms. Kora's next question. It was the nurse with Kora's nightly snack and medications.

Donovan took the opportunity to end the visit.

"Ms. Kora, we are going to head back to the house. I'll come by again soon to let you know when the funeral will be." He leaned in to hug her and kiss her on the jaw.

The kids did the same.

Jade approached the bed to say goodbye.

"I need a hug from you too, dear," Ms. Kora said.

When Jade leaned in, Ms. Kora softly whispered into her ear. "Kamill and I dreamed of you. I'm glad you are alright. Come back to see me."

Ms. Kora's words sent chills throughout Jade's body. Ms. Kora released her and then said loudly enough for everyone to hear, "Donnie, thank you for bringing her to meet me."

As they left the room, Jade was visibly shaken.

"Are you okay?" Donovan asked.

"No."

Donovan stopped walking and grabbed Jade's hand, "What's wrong?"

"Ms. Kora said that she and Kamill dreamed about me and she is glad that I'm okay."

"Jade, it's the gift of dreams. Ms. Kora and Kamill sometimes share dreams. I can't explain it. She'll have to explain it to you."

"Okay," was her only reply.

Chapter Twelve

Four days later Donovan's parents, his sister, Jade's mom, the twins, and Ms. Evelyn flew into Hartsfield-Jackson Atlanta International Airport and arrived at Donovan's house in the late afternoon. Gavin and Sydnee arrived shortly after everyone else.

There was a natural bond between Kamia and Kamill and their siblings, one that time could not alter or erase. The reunion with the twins and bonding with new family members felt surreal to Natalie and Khalil. From the expressions on their faces, everyone could tell that they were overwhelmed with joy and love.

Natalie asked Donovan, "Is this real or am I dreaming? It feels like a dream."

"No, sweetie, it is not a dream. All these people are now your family. I know it will take some time getting used to it, but they'll be patient."

"It's a little scary," Natalie responded.

"Yeah, it would be for me too," Donovan said.

"What should I call your parents?" Khalil asked.

"Whatever you are comfortable with," Donovan replied.

"Do you think they mind if we call them Grandmamma and Granddad?"

"No, I think they'll like that."

"What about Ms. Evelyn?"

"The girls call her Granny, but she will answer to Ms. Evelyn. No one will be offended if you call them Mr. or Ms. versus Granny, Auntie, or Uncle. Right now, everyone is here to give you the support you need. Okay?"

"Thanks, Uncle D."

*****

The service and the repass were difficult for the children. When it was over, Jade found the twins, Natalie, and Khalil sitting in the very back of the church's dining hall. Their faces were full of fear and sadness.

Jade was frustrated with herself for not being as attentive to the children as she should have. Today's events caused her mind to wander back to a place of extreme sadness. She'd hid in the women's restroom for about fifteen minutes.

"Hey," Jade said to the children. "I think it's time for us to go home. Wait here and I'll be right back."

She needed to find her mother and Donovan to let them know that it was time for them to leave. Jade found her mom, Ms. Evelyn, and Sharron greeting and thanking the guests for coming. She informed them that the children were ready to go home and asked Ms. Evelyn to take the kids to the foyer. She searched the room for Donovan and found him talking to a group of attractive women. Although Jade approached Donovan from behind, he turned, as if knowing she was near.

Donovan immediately recognized the anxiety in her eyes and body language. He excused himself from the guests.

"The kids are emotionally drained and I would like to take them home," Jade said. "The kids don't want to ride in the limo, so I am driving Gavin's Yukon. My mom and Ms. Evelyn will go with me. I'll expect you home by six...not a minute later.

"This has been a hard day for all of us. Your mom will stay with Amelia. I don't think Amelia should be alone tonight. Bring her to the house. Tell her that she can stay in the main house or the guest house. I just don't want her out here in Marrietta alone.

"Mom and Ms. Evelyn are with the kids in the foyer. Please come give them hugs and kisses. Khalil may resist, but he needs a hug from you. You have to help him with this, Donovan. This kind of hurt and grief can be overwhelming for an adult, so just imagine for a child how difficult it is. Death has visited the kids and their family more than most."

Donovan could have sworn that Jade spoke all of this in one breath. Everything she said was in statements, not to be questioned or challenged. He knew that she was sincerely concerned about the kids. But Jade's emotions were heightened for other reasons and he was concerned for her, as well.

He leaned down, kissed her lips, and said, "You are absolutely right. No later than six, and bring Amelia. Thank you, sweetheart."

They walked hand in hand to the front of the church.

*****

At the house, Jade, her mom, and Ms. Evelyn sat in the sunroom drinking iced tea after successfully getting the children to lie down for a nap.

"Jade, how long do you plan on staying in Atlanta?" her mom asked. "Are you able to work on the Holly Garden project from here?"

Jade knew the underlying question was, "What is going on between you and Donovan?"

As she searched for an answer, her mother stated, "Donovan has arranged for me to fly back to Hawaii on Thursday. I'll only be here for three more days, but I'll help in any way that I can."

Jade stared out of the window. She had no answers for the many "whys," "how longs," or "what's next" questions. She opened her mouth and the words in her heart spilled out.

"Everything has been a whirlwind around me. But I want to be *here* with Donovan and the children. I cannot leave them. Donovan and I have not discussed anything. I think we both realize that the reality of all that has happened is very overwhelming. He hasn't asked me to leave, nor has he asked me to stay. But I believed in my heart that this is where *I need to be.*"

"Jade, from the outside looking in, this does appear to be a whirlwind," her mom said. "There are four precious children involved. Everything that I taught you about loving and giving shows in the way that you have cared for these children over the past few days. I am very proud of you. But these children need consistency in their lives. Can you give them consistency?

Jade, as a mother, all I've ever wanted for you was happiness. As women, we tell ourselves and teach our daughters to marry the man that loves us the most, not the one that you love the most. The love that you and Donovan shared was so strong that it consumed you both. Your mind only allowed you to believe that *you loved him the most*, but truth be told, *you both loved each other the most*. Your relationship with Donovan is worth exploring, but you need to talk to Donovan about Holly Gardens. He will understand and support what you are doing there. Jade, look at me…You will have to finish that chapter in your life before you get too deep into this one."

Ms. Evelyn finally spoke. "Amen."

Jade couldn't speak because of the river of tears that flowed down her face. She knew she and Donovan were indeed worth exploring.

*****

Later that night, Jade couldn't sleep. The clock read 1:30 a.m. She picked up the phone and called her sister.

"Hey, sis. What are you doing up?" Onyx asked.

"I can't sleep. My thoughts and emotions are all over the place. Nathan's funeral was today."

"I know. I talked to mom and Tia earlier. I figured you were pretty busy with the children."

"I'm never too busy to talk to my sister."

Onyx was certain that Jade was crying. "Jade, Jade, talk to me."

"Onyx I want to be here with Donovan and the children, it feels so right. But I don't want to cause more harm. I have my own issues."

"Jade, I have to be honest with you, and I hope that you're not offended."

Jade sat up, because usually when Onyx prefaced a sentence

with *I don't want to offend*, she usually did.

"What you've experienced is grief over the loss of your baby and your husband. Jonothan was a wonderful man and he loved you dearly. You loved him too, but to be honest, we both know that you never stopped loving Donovan. I think after everything that happened, it was easier for you to not look back or even acknowledge that your love for him ever existed. I know you have never forgotten his birthday. Every year on his birthday, you baked a cake."

"I don't."

"Yeah, you do. I know because I've called you over the years.

"Onyx, I loved Jonothan very much. I …"

"Jade, I know that you loved Jonothan. I would never minimize your love for him or the value of your marriage. But you've been given a second chance to love the man you've carried in your spirit all these years. That's a blessing. I would give anything to just see the face of the man I carry in my spirit every day.

"What man? Whose face? What are you talking about?" Jade asked.

"No one. This conversation is about you."

"Onyx, I can't believe you're keeping something from me."

"Jade, not now. I can't talk about him." Onyx took a deep breath.

"I miss you," Jade said.

"I miss you too. So, what are you going to do about Donovan and the children?" Onyx asked.

"I want to stay."

"Then stay. Family is who we choose and who chooses us. That's what grandmamma always told us," Onyx responded.

"Onyx, thank you, and I love you."

"You're welcome and I love you more."

After hanging up the phone with Onyx, Jade heard a familiar sound. She looked out the window and saw Natalie playing basketball.

Her heart went out to the young lady. Jade too had lost her father when she was a teenager. The difference for Jade was that she still had her mother. She couldn't imagine experiencing so much loss at such a young age.

Jade dressed and walked out of the house. She stood back and watched Natalie, waiting for the perfect opportunity to join her. The ball bounced in Jade's direction.

"Check," she said. "First to 10 is the winner."

"No, I'm finished," Natalie said.

Jade knew that Natalie needed to play longer and decided to push. "Please, I can't sleep. Besides, I hope you are not scared to play an old lady."

Natalie laughed. "Jade, you are far from old; I just…"

Jade threw the ball to her and said, "Oh come on, check or chicken."

The basketball player in Natalie surfaced and she agreed.

Jade and Natalie played three games before they called it a night.

"Let's go shower and share a late night snack." Jade rattled off a list of snack options. They both agreed on a peanut butter and jelly sandwich with a glass of milk.

*****

Donovan watched Natalie shoot hoops from the kitchen window. He was tempted to go outside to join her when Jade appeared from the shadows. Natalie responded to Jade.

He smiled as he thought about the plan that he came up with Tia, Onyx to reunite with Jade. But God had the last laugh in this situation. His timing was perfect. Natalie needed Jade, and in many ways Jade needed Natalie. Jade knew better than anyone about the pain of grieving the death of a loved one, as well as the journey to healing.

Donovan walked back to the bedroom when he heard Jade and Natalie enter the kitchen. He didn't want them to know that he had been watching them.

*****

Jade made Natalie and herself sandwiches, poured two glasses of milk, and placed their food on top of the island, so they could sit next to each other. "This is one of my favorite snacks," Jade shared.

"Mine too. Thank you," Natalie said.

Jade reached for Natalie's hand and said grace.

"You're welcome," Jade responded.

"I like that last shot you made. Who taught you how to play?" Natalie asked.

"My dad taught me and my sister, Onyx. My dad taught us a lot of things. He died when I was 18. I was older than you, but I still remember the pain like it was yesterday."

"Was he sick?"

"Yes, he died from liver cancer. It was so hard watching him suffer."

Natalie sighed and then spoke, her voice trembling. "It was horrible and there was nothing we could do. Amelia was great. She could have walked away, but she didn't. I am thankful for her. I've never felt pain like this before."

"Natalie, we are all here to help you. We could never replace your dad in your heart, but we can help you through this. It is a lifelong process, but we are here."

Natalie cried and Jade held her until she stopped. They moved to the family room and reclined on the chaise lounge.

*****

It was there that Donovan found them asleep hours later. Jade cradled Natalie close; it was the perfect picture. He kissed and covered them both with a blanket.

Donovan returned to his room and reflected on the day. He thought of Ms. Kora. She had decided not to attend the funeral service. She told Donovan, "I see Nathan and my daughter every night in my dreams. I don't have to see his body stretched out in a box to know he has passed on."

He thought of the children, Jade, and the challenges that

they might face in the future. Donovan kneeled at the side of his bed and prayed for strength and for God to prepare his heart and mind for whatever was ahead.

Chapter Thirteen

J ade and Donovan talked with Natalie and Khalil about choosing a way to memorialize Nathan's death. They explained that by establishing a ritual, it would help them grieve. Natalie and Khalil agreed to take flowers to the grave site once a month.

Jade was well aware that unresolved grief caused emotional and physical stagnation. She would do everything in her power to help Natalie and Khalil develop the appropriate coping skills for dealing with their father's death. She talked with Donovan about bereavement counseling for Natalie and Khalil, and provided him with the name of three licensed clinical social workers in the area, who specialized in grief and bereavement counseling for children.

Donovan and Jade spoke together with the kids to share their thoughts. "Jade and I think that you both would benefit from bereavement counseling," Donovan said. "What do you think?"

Unexpectedly, Natalie spoke with quiet confidence. "Kamia said that you were at St. Simons when...well, you know, before my dad died. She said it was nice there. Will you take us there? I just need to..." Then the dam broke as the tears and the sobs began.

Donovan kneeled in front of both children and said, "We can go anywhere you want."

Natalie looked at Jade and asked, "Will you come with us?"

"Yes, of course. But you both have to promise to always tell Donovan what you are feeling. The next few months will be full of new and different experiences, but we're here to help you," Jade said, kissing her forehead.

There was a knock on the study door. Kamill and Kamia walked in without waiting for a "come in."

"Natalie, are you okay?" the twins asked in one voice.

"Yes, I'm okay," she said, wiping her face.

"Don't cry," Kamia reached up to help Natalie wipe her tears. Kamia smiled then added, "God made sisters for sharing laughter and wiping tears."

They laughed at Kamia's imitation of her Nana Pearl. Donovan and Jade exchanged eye contact, both wondering when the kids started referring to her mom as "Nana Pearl."

Pearl and Ms. Evelyn appeared at the door, curious about the family discussion.

Jade spoke first, "Natalie and Khalil would like to go to St. Simons for a while."

"We could leave as early as this coming Saturday," Donovan added.

"Hmm," Ms. Evelyn said.

"Well, if Ms. Evelyn is up to it, I think that she and I could take the kids as early as Tuesday evening. We'll go get settled in and you could join us on Saturday," Pearl said.

"Pearl, I thought you were leaving Wednesday," Ms. Evelyn responded.

"Nana Pearl, are you staying with us?" Kamia asked.

"Yes, precious. Nana Pearl has decided to stay longer."

"Well, yes, I am up to it," Ms. Evelyn said. "Donovan, this will give you and Jade some time to finalize the renovation plans with the contractor and resolve several other issues."

Jade knew what the women were up to and was about to speak when her mom interrupted her.

"Ms. Evelyn, I think that is a great idea. Let's leave the work for Jade and Donovan, while we go have fun in the sun with the kids."

"I agree. Okay, kids, who wants a snack?"

Natalie and Khalil stayed behind to finish their talk with Donovan about counseling.

"Uncle Donovan, can we start counseling when we get back from St. Simons Island?" Khalil asked.

"Yes, that's fine with me. Natalie, what do you think?" Donovan asked.

"That's fine with me," she replied nonchalantly.

"Okay. Go get your snack," Jade said.

Jade and Donovan followed the children downstairs, but then walked outside.

"Donovan, Natalie doesn't seem open to the idea of counseling," Jade said.

"I know, but I think they both need it," he responded. "They are young and have lost both parents. They've had to integrate themselves into this family, this house, and our lives. All of this is overwhelming to me as an adult. I pray for strength and wisdom in this, Jade. Thank you for being here."

*****

Two days later, after everyone left for St. Simons, Donovan and Jade withdrew Khalil and Natalie from their high school and enrolled them at Tyler Academy for Higher Education. Donovan was frustrated with all the red tape and the hoops they had to jump through. It was close to four o'clock when they finished.

They ate an early dinner at one of Jade's favorite restaurants, Copeland's.

"Donovan, do you mind walking through and shopping a little at the Cumberland Mall?" Jade asked afterward.

"That's fine. It will help us digest all the food we just ate."

As they walked through the mall, Donovan asked, "What are we shopping for?"

"I just wanted to pick up a few things for me and the children. Do you need anything?" she asked.

"I wasn't aware of anything the kids needed. Did Ms. Evelyn mention anything to you?"

"She just mentioned that Natalie and Khalil packed light. That's all."

"Okay. Well, I should add you as an authorized user on my credit card if you're going to be buying things for the children."

"Donovan, that won't be necessary."

"Honey, please allow me to do this."

"No, I prefer to pay."

"Jade, listen, please. I know that you'll never take advantage of me. Please at least take this credit card to make purchases for the kids from this point on."

Jade silently agreed by nodding her head. Jade reached for the card and placed it inside her purse. She had no intentions of using the card, but to pacify Donovan, she smiled and said, "Thank you."

"You're welcome." He kissed her lips softly. "Please excuse me, while I call the credit card company."

"I'll be in Bath and Body Works."

"Okay, I'll just be a few minutes," he replied.

Jade picked up a lavender chamomile travel set and sugar scrub hand soap and lotion from Bath and Body Works. Donovan reappeared at Jade's side when she exited the store. Placing his hand on the small of her back, he said, "I added you to my credit card account. Your card should arrive in the mail in a few days."

Jade smiled, but had no intention of using Donovan's card. And he sensed this as much.

"Honey, you agreed to use the card right?" he asked.

Jade reluctantly responded, "Yes."

"Alright, since we have that settled, can we make a quick stop at Macy's? I need to pick up a few things."

"Okay. Macy's has a great sale right now. I think that I have a 20% off coupon," Jade said.

Donovan laughed. "Jade, are you serious?"

"Yes."

"Smart woman. You could always stretch a dollar," he whispered as he kissed her softly.

Jade purred.

Donovan purchased three packs of Ralph Lauren white T-shirts and two sets of Ralph Lauren pajama short sets with Jade's coupon.

Jade picked up hand soap and lotion from Bath and Body Works, shopped at Aéropostale, Justice, The Gap, and Old

Navy, and picked up a half dozen Cinnabons. Donovan was delighted that lately she had been eating to her heart's content.

On the drive back to the house, Jade felt like this was a good time to talk to Donovan about her work. She didn't know how long she was going to stay with him and his family, but she couldn't forget about the project she had started to memorialize Jonothan.

"Donovan, I've been meaning to talk more about my job and what I do in Summer, but everything has happened so quickly. I am the Executive Director of Holly Health and Community Services Center, which Jonothan, Emanuel, and I founded. The center provides medical care, mental health counseling, and enrichment programs to low-income families in Summer, Georgia. Since Jon....well, I've been working on another project named Holly Gardens. Holly Gardens will be a multi-use community within a three-mile radius of the Holly Health and Community Services Center. The goal of the project is to renovate and repair the homes at the heart of the community. In addition, the plan will include building a low-income housing complex with 200 units, a community park, community sport complex, and retail shops."

Donovan's eyes bulged open wide.

"Yes, I always dream big."

He smiled, "I admire and respect that quality in you. Is there anything I can do to help?"

"No, not really. But enough about me, let's talk about renovating your beautiful home," Jade said.

Donovan shared his ideas and asked Jade for input. Jade suggested that the guest room located in the basement be redecorated into a sports theme for Khalil. She also thought that it would be glad to add more rooms to include: a game room, movie room, and a half bathroom. Jade thought the family room and kitchen should be expanded also. Natalie and Ms. Evelyn both enjoyed cooking, and the current layout did not allow for two cooks to maneuver comfortably.

The bedrooms located on the upper level would only

require redecorating. Jade suggested decorating Natalie's room using a café or bistro theme with a mural of an Italian bistro as an accented wall. Jade thought it would be nice to redecorate the twins' room and Donovan's office, also.

Donovan liked the suggestions Jade offered. He'd wanted to make the house more of a home for them--Jade just didn't realize that the "them" included her. He intended to share this home with her and the children that he had been blessed with.

Donovan had to catch up on some work, so once they returned home, he went to his office to try to focus. Jade went into one of the guest rooms to rest. Nathan's death had brought her back to thoughts about her own loss.

Donovan could not concentrate as he continued to think about the love he had for Jade. Although they only shared intimate words and kisses, Donovan had fallen in love with Jade again more than he'd thought possible. His feelings were real, but he'd wait for her to realize her feelings and allow her to make the first move. She was his desire and all he could imagine was making love to her with her smooth chocolate legs around him. Donovan got up from his desk and headed to his bathroom for his nightly cold shower.

With the children, Ms. Evelyn, and her mom gone, being alone in the house with Donovan had taken its toll on Jade. She wanted to join him in his room. Instead, she lay across the bed and allowed her mind to be consumed with thoughts of him. She inhaled deeply, remembering his scent, a combination of his cologned body wash and the masculine smell that was uniquely his. She imagined lying in his arms with her head on his chest. She imagined kissing the trail of hair down to his stomach and the taste of him. She imagined him spooning her with his hand resting on that sensitive area on her hip. She smiled, thinking of his hairy legs intertwined with hers. She laughed at the thought of him taunting her for still sleeping with one socked foot. She imagined them lying facing one another, with him asleep, as she stared at her first true love. She imagined them lying so close it felt as if his heart was beating inside of her and sharing an intimacy that transcended from the simple gesture of touching the man she loved.

No words were required for the existence of a love as powerful as Eros love. The intensity of her craving for him was beyond anything she had ever experienced. With thoughts of him, Jade pleasured herself again and again until she drifted into sleep.

Chapter Fourteen

The following day, Donovan and Jade met with Carl, the CEO of CC and J Construction Company. It was the same construction company that built Donovan's home two years earlier. Donovan wanted the renovations to be completed in six months at the most. Jade thought Donovan's expectations were unreasonable, but he was not willing to negotiate the timeframe. CC and J would be responsible for the renovations and Jade would be responsible for redecorating.

Donovan chose the renovation plans that Jade favored. He thought a home should reflect the warmth and atmosphere of a woman's heart. Independent of size and expenses, without a woman's heart, a house was merely wood and stone. He prayed that Jade's heart would be the warmth in his family's home.

Donovan called and gave Ms. Evelyn a brief update on the meeting with the contractor. He told her that they would have to move into the guest house until the renovations were complete. He and Jade would arrive in St. Simons on Saturday morning, as planned.

"How is Jade?"

"She's wonderful. We shopped for the kids yesterday. She's in her room, probably asleep by now."

"Pearl and I were hoping that you two would spend this time *together*, talking about your relationship. Has that happened?"

Donovan was very much aware of what Ms. Evelyn's *together* meant. "No, but we've used our time together wisely. When Jade says she wants to talk about us, we will. Until then, I am just following her lead. She hasn't talked about her husband or daughter yet. She'll talk in her own time. I'm just thankful for this time with her. Good night and kiss the kids for me," he said.

Donovan turned on the radio and headed to his bathroom for another cold shower.

*****

Jade stood outside of Donovan's bedroom door for the second time that night. The first time she'd come to him, he was in the shower. She'd taken that as a sign and returned to her room and called Tia.

"Hey, I just wanted to thank you for lunch today."

"You're welcome. I enjoy your company. So why are you really calling?" Tia asked.

"Donovan and I had a great night. We cooked dinner together. It was fun. He is the same in so many ways, but different too. He is different in ways that I would never imagine."

"Okay, so what's bothering you? Are the differences that you notice in him an issue for you?"

"No, it's nothing like that," Jade replied.

"Jade, what is it?"

"It's me. When I look up into his eyes, I am consumed. He makes me feel like I am the most important person in the universe and my body responds like it's chocolate fondue. My body is on fire."

"Ooooww. Um hum. So is this a good time for me to say '*I told you so*'? Yeah, I think so. "

"Tia, we're still getting to know each other again, adjusting to the individuals we've become. Becoming intimate now would only complicate things. But I want to be close to him. I want to lay with him and cuddle." Jade answered.

"Jade, I completely understand. I've been celibate four years. But there is no harm in cuddling. Has he done anything to give you the impression that he won't accept cuddling?" Tia asked.

"Tia, honestly. I don't know if I can."

"It's your call, Ms. Jade."

"I know. I'll talk to you later. Good night."

Now Jade stood outside Donovan's bedroom door for the second time. They had been alone for two days, and they'd avoided the subject of their relationship. He had been the perfect gentlemen. Not once had he attempted to kiss her intimately; he'd just given good night kisses on the cheek. They'd held hands and shared intimate smiles and glances.

Jade shook her head in an attempt to clear the thoughts from her head. They needed to talk. She needed to tell him about everything in her life. But more than anything, Jade didn't want to sleep alone. She wanted to be held and caressed by him. She wanted to feel safe in his arms. Before she could change her mind, Jade knocked on the door.

Donovan was sitting in his bed watching ESPN when he heard a soft knock on the door.

"Come in."

Once his eyes absorbed the vision of Jade, his body responded immediately. How could she look so damn sexy in cotton pajamas? Donovan took a deep breath and adjusted the comforter to help conceal his erection. He was glad that he'd slipped on pajama bottoms before getting into bed. He would need another cold shower when she left his room.

Jade had not stepped into the room completely; the door knob was still in her right hand. Donovan registered the look of uncertainty in her eyes and asked gently, "Babe, are you okay? Besides missing a sock?"

Jade looked down and laughed. Donovan's question had broken the tension. He muted the TV and stretched his hand out, inviting her to join him in the bed, and she did. Donovan moved to the center of the bed. Jade sat down and moved her body parallel to Donovan's.

"What's going on?"

"I wanted to talk to you. But now, I just want you to hold me."

"Come here." He turned off the TV and hit the same remote to dim the lights. Jade joined him in the bed. He repositioned the pillows behind him and lay back with Jade in the cradle of his arms. He rested his hand on her right hip. For several minutes, he listened to her breathe. Then he spoke in a whisper.

"Jade, when you're ready to share your life with me, I am here." He kissed her forehead and pulled her closer.

Jade nodded her head in response to Donovan's statement. She snuggled closer, placed her hand on his chest, and moved her leg over his.

"Donovan, I could never give you children," Jade whispered sadly.

Donovan held her closer and gently pressed a kiss to her forehead. "God gave me four to share with you," he responded.

"Donovan."

"Yes."

"Thank you for being such a gentleman. You've been really patient and I....well."

"Baby, when the time is right, we'll both know. Until then, I'll continue to cherish every moment we have. I want you to know that I am safe. I am tested three times a year," he answered.

"Thank you, and I am safe, too ," she responded. "I haven't been with anyone since..."

"Shh, shh. Good night, sweetheart."

With the contentment of being close to one another, Jade and Donovan fell into a deep sleep. They both rested well that night.

*****

The next morning, Jade woke first. She and Donovan's bodies were in the same position. Jade gently untangled their legs, turned on her side, and pressed her bottom into Donovan's side. Donovan automatically turned his body to spoon hers. He pulled her even closer and kissed the back of her neck.

"Let's sleep late today."

"What do you consider late?"

"Nine o'clock."

She said, "Okay." Then she moved her body closer to his. She gasped this time at the hardness pressed into her bottom.

"Be still. I'm growing harder each time you move."

Jade wiggled her bottom closer to him and giggled when he groaned.

Donovan left for work at 10 a.m. He said he would be in a meeting from 11 a.m. to 1 p.m. Then he would have another meeting from 2 p.m. to 6 p.m.

They'd planned to have dinner that night, but Jade missed him and decided to surprise him with lunch. She called his cell phone, but it went straight to voicemail. That was unusual, because Donovan always answered his personal cell phone, business meeting or not. Jade prepared a fresh fruit salad, broccoli salad, turkey pitas, and sweet tea.

Jade had been to Donovan's office three times and felt comfortable finding her way. She'd only met a handful of his employees, but remembered that everyone was very polite. When Jade arrived at Donovan's office, the receptionist greeted her by name and directed her to Donovan's office. Jade knocked, but didn't get a response.

She opened the door to find a beautiful woman, who could pass for Nia Long's twin, sitting at Donovan's desk.

The woman looked up, made eye contact with Jade, and stood up. As she walked around the desk, she looked Jade up and down contemptuously. She was dressed in a tailored canary yellow linen pantsuit that complemented her statuesque frame and chocolate peep-toe sling backs.

Jade looked down at her attire. She wore a white tank top with her sorority's pink and green letters, a pair of Seven capri jeans, Sperry flip flops, Coach swing pack, and her hair was pulled back in a ponytail. Nothing about her attire said "successful businesswoman."

"I wasn't aware that he'd ordered lunch. How much is it?" the woman asked as she retrieved her Louis Vuitton purse from the conference table on the opposite side of the room.

White hot heat ran through Jade. Who the hell was this woman?

"Donovan didn't order lunch. I brought it for him and me to share. I apologize; I should have introduced myself. I'm Jade."

From the expression on the woman's face, the name meant nothing to her.

"Jade, okay, and who are you?" she responded in a catty tone.

More heat coursed through Jade. If this chick wanted to take it there, Jade would gladly escort her.

"Who I am is really none of your concern. Where is Donovan?"

As Jade completed her sentence, she heard a door open. When she looked to her left, Donovan stood there, looking absolutely gorgeous with a look of surprise and delight on his face. Jade approached him and kissed him softly and sensually.

"Hi, sweetheart. I brought you lunch," Jade said. She gave him another light kiss and glanced in the direction in which the woman was standing.

Donovan looked confused momentarily, but the tension in the room prompted his intuition and he responded.

"Thank you, sweetheart. This is a pleasant surprise and your timing is perfect. Jade, this is Daphne, an associate here at Johnson and Johnson. Daphne, please excuse me, we'll have to reschedule this meeting for later today."

Daphne gathered her belongings with a look of defeat on her face.

Jade smiled. In less than ten minutes, everyone at Johnson and Johnson would know that Donovan was spoken for. She'd clearly staked her claim.

*****

Later that evening...

Although the foundation of their love had been laid fourteen years ago, Donovan watched Jade in amazement. Her over-the-top cheering and protests during the basketball game would have annoyed some men, but it amused Donovan. She enjoyed most sports, but she had a special love for women's basketball. He had surprised her with courtside tickets to the WNBA Dreams vs. Liberty basketball game. When he called after work to invite her to the game, she'd yelled so loudly through the phone that Donovan was convinced he'd have permanent damage to his left eardrum.

She was still the same woman she was in college to the core: strong, independent, and compassionate, yet she was very different. He loved to see her stress-free. She yelled and cheered with no concern about what others thought. He would give her the world if he knew that it would bring her joy. Tonight she'd been overjoyed by the simple gesture of attending a WNBA basketball game with him.

After the game, they went to Lynnette and Eva's Soul Food Café to eat. Lynnette and Eva's Café was one of the city's hidden treasures. Jade and Donovan shared a platter of the best lemon pepper wings, hot wings, potato salad, and homemade fries Jade had ever eaten. Then for dessert they shared a slice of Ms. Eva's delicious coconut cake. When they finished, her stomach and heart were both full of contentment.

When they arrived home, Jade and Donovan walked the grounds of the estate to help their food digest. They held hands and enjoyed each other's companionship.

"Donovan, tonight was perfect," Jade said.

He chuckled, "Baby, you are perfect."

Jade leaned up and kissed him softly. "Thank you."

"You're welcome. We'd better head back to the house. We have a busy day tomorrow," Donovan said.

"What time are we leaving for St. Simons?" Jade asked.

"Is nine too early for you?"

"No, I was planning to look over some reports from Monique before we went to sleep. Are you working on anything tonight?"

"Nope, I'll watch TV while you work."

"Okay, I'll be in after I shower," Jade leaned upward and kissed Donovan passionately. The searing kiss consumed them. Donovan's body hardened instantly and Jade pressed her body closer, enjoying the hardness. "I won't be long."

"Oh." He blew out a breath and said, "I'll be waiting."

Chapter Fifteen

Whent Jade and Donovan arrived to the house in St. Simons, Ms. Pearl and Ms. Evelyn greeted them.

"How was your drive?" Ms. Evelyn asked.

"It was very pleasant," Donovan answered as he looked at Jade.

She blushed and said, "Yes, it was."

"Great," Ms. Pearl said. "Now, Ms. Evelyn and I are taking three days off. We are staying at Tia's house."

"Donovan, Pearl and I have been amazing grandmothers. Please book us a day at the spa, on you," Ms. Evelyn said.

Donovan laughed at her forwardness and said, "Yes, ma'am. Absolutely. Is there anything else you need?" He looked between the two women.

"No, just don't call us and we won't call you," Ms. Pearl said.

"No calls. Lunch at Iguana's on Thursday. Have fun," Ms. Evelyn said sarcastically.

Jade and Donovan exchanged looks and wondered what had the ladies running out of the house.

They went out onto the deck to greet the children.

"Daddy, Jade," the twins said as they greeted them with hugs.

"Hi, Uncle D and Jade," was Khalil's greeting.

"Hi," Natalie said, but she never looked up from her magazine.

Jade elbowed Donovan. Something was up.

"I need everyone in the house for a family meeting. Please go to the kitchen table," Donovan said in a fatherly tone.

All the children complied immediately.

"Ms. Evelyn and Ms. Pearl are staying at Tia's house for three days so that Jade and I can have some time with you," he announced once they were all seated at the table.

"Natalie and Khalil, how do you like St. Simons?" Jade

asked.

"It's nice," Khalil responded.

"It's okay," Natalie said.

"Good, now let's plan what we're going to do the rest of the time that we are here."

Kamia, Kamill, and Khalil started rattling off suggestions. Natalie remained distant and quiet. Donovan and Jade excused the other children from the table, but asked Natalie to stay. Donovan moved to sit next to her.

"Natalie, is there anything that you would like to do while we're here? Is there anything that you want to talk about?"

"No."

"Natalie…"

"The twins are annoying. They follow me everywhere, and they ask a thousand questions. Ms. Pearl and Ms. Evelyn wouldn't let me cook or even help with the meals. I have a lot of seafood recipe ideas that I want to try. The seafood here is fresh… Uncle D. I thought that I would feel better being away from Atlanta, but the pain followed me." Natalie's voice cracked and she exhaled, tears silently running down her face.

Jade got up to retrieve a Kleenex and handed it to Natalie.

"Natalie, I wish that I could take the pain away, but I can't," Donovan said. "I am here to help you grieve and heal until the pain doesn't hurt so badly. I know your dad was a great father and he adored you."

"I know that he did. I miss him so much. Khalil is walking around all happy-go-lucky. That makes me mad! Why isn't he sad? He acts like nothing has happened."

Khalil had overheard. He entered the room and sat across from his sister. "That's not true. I miss him too, but I'm staying busy, while you stay cooped up in this house."

"Leave me alone," Natalie snapped back.

"No. It's the truth and you know it. You've been mean and snappy. I can take it, but the twins can't. You need to apologize," Khalil retorted.

"Do you owe them an apology?" Donovan asked.

Natalie sighed. "Yeah, I guess so."

"Khalil, go get your sisters and bring them in here," Donovan said.

Kamill and Kamia walked in holding hands. Khalil stood next to them.

"Have a seat please."

"Daddy, we haven't done anything. We were about to, but we didn't," Kamia said.

"Kamia, shh, don't say anything," Kamill said.

"Don't say what?" Donovan asked, "What are you two up to?"

They didn't respond.

"Kamill, Kamia answer me, now." Donovan's voice was stern.

"Well, we were going to pour hair oil in Natalie's basketball shoes," Kamill said.

Khalil laughed.

"You what?" Jade asked before she realized it.

"She's mean to us," Kamia answered.

"She yells at us and tells us to go away," Kamill added.

"She doesn't like us," Kamia said.

All eyes were on Natalie. She seemed shocked by the girls' comments.

"Girls, Natalie is still very sad and sometimes sad feelings can make people say things they don't mean," Jade explained.

"I'm sorry," Natalie said, beginning to cry. "You're my sisters and I love you."

"Are you sure? It doesn't feel like love," Kamill said.

"Yes," Natalie answered.

"Natalie, don't cry. I forgive you," Kamia said, hugging her sister.

"Me too," Kamill replied.

"Thank you," Natalie said, hugging both of her sisters.

"Listen, we're all still learning each other's personalities and how to adjust to one another and to Nathan being gone,"

Donovan said. "When we get to Atlanta, we will begin family therapy."

"Therapy?" Natalie repeatedly asked with uncertainty.

"Yes, therapy," Jade answered.

"We need help with everything," Kamia said.

"Khalil, twins, you may be excused," Donovan said.

When the girls and Khalil left again, Jade turned to Natalie. "Now is there anything else that you want to talk about?" she asked.

"Yes, I want to cook. Ms. Pearl and Ms. Evelyn wouldn't let me."

"I know, let's talk about your recipe ideas," Donovan said.

Natalie shared her ideas with Jade and Donovan. She made a list of items that she needed from the seafood market and Publix grocery store.

Donovan agreed to take her shopping for what she needed. If cooking would help her grieve, then so be it.

*****

As planned, everyone met for lunch at Iguana's Seafood Restaurant on Thursday. Afterward, they walked downtown and window shopped, and then walked to Yobe Frozen Yogurt for a cool treat.

"Let's head to the pier and sit for while," Donovan said, leading the way.

"Can we walk over to the park?" Khalil asked.

"Yeah," Donovan answered.

"Can we go?" Kamia asked.

"Sure, come on," Khalil answered.

"You, go on too," Ms. Pearl instructed Natalie.

"Be careful," Ms. Evelyn yelled.

The adults sat and watched the kids play and explore to their hearts content. Khalil was talking with some of the teens that he'd met from the island while glancing between the twins. Natalie was swinging.

"There is a serene feeling that lingers over this island,"

Pearl said.

"Yes, there is," Ms. Evelyn responded.

"Um hum," Jade said snuggling against Donovan.

"Pearl, when are you flying back to Hawaii?" Evelyn asked.

"When I return to Atlanta, Jade is dropping me off at the airport. I've got to get back and get Onyx back on track," Pearl responded.

Jade laughed.

"Don't laugh, Jade. Your sister is letting life pass her by flying that dang helicopter."

"Mom!"

"Don't 'Mom' me."

Donovan stood, and the women turned their eyes to see what had captured his attention. A handsome young man was talking to Natalie and she was all smiles. Donovan began walking in their direction when Ms. Pearl intercepted him.

"No, Donovan. You can't react everytime you see her talking with a boy. You have to trust her to make good choices," she said, squeezing his forearm.

"I was an overprotective older brother with Danielle. I can't imagine how many gray hairs I will get from fathering a teenage girl. This is new for me."

"Yes, it is, but you will have to learn to handle situations like this appropriately, or she'll alienate you. Jade's father, God rest his soul, was overprotective of Jade and Onyx, but eventually he found an even balance. I suggest that you do the same," Ms. Pearl said, guiding him back to sit beside Jade.

Pearl winked at Jade and Evelyn.

*****

Jade and Donovan eventually settled into a routine with the children. Kamill, Kamia, Natalie, and Khalil's personalities continued to clash from time to time, as expected.

Donovan made it a priority to spend individual time with each child daily. He and Khalil would jog on the beach or play video games. He taught Kamia to swim, and he and

Kamill looked for seashells each day. In the evenings, he and Natalie cooked dinner. Throughout their time together, he and Jade would steal kisses and late night talks.

Natalie used the time to organize her family recipes. She had grown up cooking with her grandmother. Before Ms. Kora moved into the assisted living facility, she gave Natalie the family's recipes of four generations. Natalie was typing up both the original recipes and her modified versions of the recipes. Her goal was to develop a cookbook.

Khalil spent his time playing basketball, biking, or swimming with the guys he had met on the island. He decided to try out for the basketball team at the new school. Donovan and Khalil began to divide their time together between jogging and basketball.

After a late night game of basketball, Khalil told Donovan, "You know, for as long as I can remember, basketball has always been me and my dad's thing to do together. So, since he died, I haven't really wanted to play. So sharing that time with you tonight was hard, but it's cool, thanks.

"Thanks for at least letting me try."

Nathan had been a great father. Donovan knew it would take time for Natalie and Khalil to find a comfortable space for him in their hearts. He also knew that it would take him time adjust to Natalie and Khalil being part of his family. Donovan prayed for the wisdom to bind his new family together.

Chapter Sixteen

The family returned from St. Simons two weeks later and moved into the guest house temporarily. The renovations to the main house were on schedule. The day after their return, the family went to the nursing home to celebrate Ms. Kora's sixty-fifth birthday.

Ms. Kora was overjoyed to have all of her grandchildren together.

The twins, however, had a difficult time adjusting to sharing their time with Ms. Kora with Natalie and Khalil. Donovan had taken the twins to visit Ms. Kora at least twice a month for the past five years, and they too shared a very special bond with her. The twins called Ms. Kora "Mimi," whereas Natalie and Khalil called her "Grandma."

"Mimi, why do you let them call you Grandma?" Kamia asked.

"Because your sister and brother have always called me Grandma."

"Well, I like Mimi better, don't you?" Kamia continued.

"I like seeing all of your faces together, little girl. I prayed for the day when I would have all of my daughter's children together again."

She reached for Donovan's hand and said, "Thank you, Donnie."

*****

The day after Ms. Kora's birthday party, Donovan traveled to his North Carolina, Colorado, and Texas corporate offices to finalize several plans. He had been gone for five days. With Donovan away, Jade thought about the responsibilities that awaited her in Summer, Georgia, and the Holly Gardens project. She briefly mentioned the project to Donovan, but she didn't tell him that the project was to memorialize Jonothan's legacy. Her mother's words rang clear, "You will have to finish that chapter of your life before you start this one."

Well, too late, this one was no longer a chapter, but a book. Jade didn't want to leave Donovan or the children. But she needed to finish the project and release the guilt from moving on from Jonothan. She needed to tell Donovan about the painful memories she kept in her secret place and release the guilt that she carried for fourteen years. She loved Donovan and wanted to start a life with him. Jade was overcome with emotions. She needed to hear Donovan's voice to help her calm the emotional storms within her.

Jade attempted to call Donovan, but his phone went straight to voicemail. She tried the call again and it yielded the same results. Jade threw the phone on her bed, grabbed a pillow, and yelled silently into it, until her silent yells became silent tears.

*****

After being away for five days, Donovan missed his family. He was looking forward to surprising them all this evening. He ended his business trip early and hoped to be home in time for dinner. He purchased nice gifts for everyone. He bought beautiful topaz and silver jewelry for Jade, Ms. Evelyn, and the girls. He got Khalil a nice pair of cowboy boots with a matching belt.

During the flight, Donovan thought about his relationship with Jade. She was a wonderful person, and it was a privilege to have her in his life. She naturally assumed the role of mother to the children and that was important to him. Everyone seemed to be comfortable and settled into a routine, like one big, happy family. He needed to talk to Jade about their relationship. He didn't know whether or not Jade would be returning back home or if she would stay with him. One thing was for sure, and that was they could not continue to play house. It was not fair to everyone involved, especially the kids. School was scheduled to start August 12th, which was less than three weeks away.

Since the flight was delayed due to weather, he arrived home after 9:30 p.m. To Donovan's amazement, the house was quiet. He thought that they were all asleep until he found a note from Jade.

Ms. Evelyn,

I hope the kids enjoyed the movie. I am at the main house working on some things. I'll be in late. Call me if you need me.

Jade

Donovan went to check on Jade and found her painting an accented wall in Natalie's room. She was listening to her iPod and singing along to Tamia's "I Can't Get Enough of You." He smiled, watching her body move to the lyrics of the song. He approached her slowly, not wanting to frighten her.

Jade knew the moment that Donovan entered the room; desire stirred within her body and white heat surged through her in response to his proximity. She closed her eyes and fought to control her breathing as she anticipated his touch. When he pressed his sculpted chest against her back, his hardness rested against her buttocks. His hand wrapped around hers, removed the paint brush from her hand, placed it in the paint pan, and turned her into his arms. He placed a kiss on her lips and rested his hands on her hips.

"I thought we both agreed that the contractor would paint, not you. Why are you out here so late, alone?"

Jade decided to be honest with Donovan. She missed him, desired him, and wanted to make her body one with his. She loved him and his children. Well, maybe she wouldn't say anything about love yet.

"I miss you when you're away . . . especially today. I called, but you didn't answer. I was frustrated and decided to use my time and energy wisely. The room needed more work, so..."

"You missed me," he replied, surprised by Jade's admission. Although he'd known that she loved him and the kids, he allowed her to dictate the terms of their relationship.

As her hands slid from his chest to his neck, Jade responded, "Yes, I missed you. I can't pretend that I don't feel this love story happening between us. It's real. Thank you for being patient with me. I love you, Donovan Johnson...." She had said love out loud and it lingered in the air, but Jade didn't care. Life had given her another chance to love and she'd taken it. She cupped Donovan's head and brought him closer until their lips met. The kiss was full of all the passion that she'd suppressed.

Once she released his mouth from captivity, Donovan said in a deep, throaty voice, "I love you more."

"Show me," she said, low and seductively, as she pressed her body closer to him.

Donovan moaned at the intense pleasure of her body pressed hard against him. "Baby, are you sure?"

"Yes, make love to me."

Donovan lifted Jade and she wrapped her legs around his waist. He carried her to the master bathroom as she kissed and nibbled his neck. Jade slid down his length and gasped at his hardness.

The removal of their clothing and their shower was a blur through their sensual kisses and caresses.

Now as they walked hand in hand into the master bedroom, Jade experienced a strong sensation of desire and fear. She hadn't been intimate with a man since Jonothan's death.

Donovan felt an immediate change in her. He placed her on the edge of the bed and positioned himself between her legs. He rested his head on her forehead and said in a gentle tone, "I love you with all my heart. I'll wait--"

"No! I want you. Donovan, I need you," Jade said, as she pulled him closer until her center made contact with his hardness. She moaned at the contact, barely able to contain the fire burning inside her. She kissed the corners of

Donovan's mouth, using the tip of her tongue to outline his top and bottom lips. He tasted good, and she wanted more. She broke the kiss and slid up further in the bed. "Come here."

Donovan moved closer to her, but instead of touching her, he opened the nightstand drawer and retrieved several condoms. When he turned around, Jade was lying down on the bed as she looked up at him. Donovan thought how beautiful she was as he licked his lips with anticipation of the kiss. Donovan pulled her closer to him and Jade captured his tongue and sucked it until he heard himself groan.

She moved her hand to massage his hard thickness and heard Donovan's sharp intake of breath. She kissed a slow trail down his neck, giving attention to his chest and nipples, and then his stomach. Jade marveled at the sight, scent, and feel of him as she lowered her mouth to take him in.

Donovan felt like his head was spinning and his body would erupt from the pure bliss her mouth evoked against his skin. Memories of her passionate and uninhibited lovemaking skills flooded his mind.

"Baby, stop...no." His voice was heavy and raspy. He reached down and gently pulled her to him. He kissed her passionately, and their tongues continued their mating dance as he thought of her unselfish desire to please him. He gripped her bottom and she moaned as he methodically positioned her beneath him. He kissed her neck and earlobes, whispering to her as he caressed her full breasts.

He broke the kiss and said, "Hold them together for me." He sucked, licked, and feasted on her breasts, giving equal time to both. The moans and faint whimpers that escaped Jade's lips only fed the fire within him.

The sensation that coiled from her breasts to the core of her womanhood couldn't have been more wonderful. She was saturated with heated moisture between her legs from Donovan's words of love. He was now a verbal lover, one who gave instructions and provided details of what was to come. But when Donovan reached down and stroked her intimately, Jade was lost. She closed her eyes and whispered, "Please."

Donovan hissed at the contact. His fingers found her hot, fully aroused, and flowing. His hands explored her folds and sought her hidden treasures. He rubbed her hard bud and slipped one finger inside. She was hot, wet, and tight. He rubbed her more until her pleas and moans were no longer whispers.

Donovan slid another finger inside her tightness and the scent of her filled his nostrils. "Baby, your smell... damn, I need a taste." Donovan kissed his way down her body and repositioned himself. He made love to Jade with his lips, tongue, and fingers. He savored the taste and scent of her, hoping to drink from her pleasure fountain for a lifetime. He felt her body begin to spasm and she yelled his name. He continued to kiss and stroke her until both her mind and body spiraled back to earth.

As Jade lay panting and moaning from her love journey, Donovan prepared himself, protecting them both. When she opened her eyes, a reflection of love and passion were in their depths. She looked beautifully sedated.

Donovan kissed her gently and entered her in one swift stroke. She was tight and Donovan didn't move . . . he couldn't move. He allowed for her body to adjust to the length and width of him. He didn't move until he regained control of his body. He threw his head back, making a sound similar to a growl, as he began moving in and out of her with a restrained pace.

He was holding back, but she wanted and needed all of him. She lifted her hips to meet and challenge each thrust. She whispered erotic love messages and instructions, never breaking eye contact with Donovan. "Love me. I want all of you," Jade said as she positioned her feet flat on his chest to allow him deeper access.

Donovan surrendered his body. They made love long and hard with a sincere intimacy.

Shortly after their love session, Donovan unwrapped himself from Jade and said, "I'm going to run us a bath. It will help with the soreness. You haven't used those muscles in a while."

"You're right, but I plan to use them a lot more, tonight and early morning," Jade said.

Donovan smiled at this sensual and uninhibited side of Jade.

Chapter Seventeen

It had been raining for the past two days and the children were bored with being indoors. Jade loved rainy days, as some of her fondest memories were from days like today. Her mom would make warm hot chocolate with whipped cream and sprinkles for her and Onyx. Then they played board games or watched Disney classics. Her parents considered rainy days the perfect opportunity for family time and "good ole' fashioned fun."

So that's exactly what Jade had planned for their evening. She ordered pizza, cheese sticks, wings, and cinnamon sticks. She'd already purchased classic family games: Chutes and Ladders, Hungry Hippo, Connect Four, Operation, UNO, Sorry, and Monopoly.

When Donovan got up to refill his glass of lemonade, he decided to get his camera from his office. Spending time together as a family was what life-long memories were made of and he wanted to capture those moments. He quietly stood in the doorway of the kitchen and took pictures of his family.

Ms. Evelyn insisted that he sit down and that she snap pictures of Donovan with his family. Ms. Evelyn was overjoyed by the perfect scene that played out before her eyes.

She was pulled from her thoughts by the ringing of the telephone.

"Hello, Ms. Evelyn, this is Gavin. Is Donovan near you?"

"Yes, he's right here. What is it, Gavin?" She instinctively knew something was wrong by the tone of Gavin's voice.

"Someone broke into Danielle's house tonight. She is okay. I'm sure Donovan will explain everything once we get off the phone."

"Donovan, it's Gavin." The tone of Ms. Evelyn's voice prompted Donovan to move swiftly to the phone and out of the dining room.

Donovan listened to Gavin as he walked to his office.

Someone had broken into Danielle's home while Gavin, Danielle, and Sydnee were out bowling. He'd dropped Sydnee off at a friend's house before taking Danielle home.

The alarm system had notified the police, and when they arrived at Danielle's house, the police were already there. Danielle had missed their calls, since her phone was set on vibrate. Her laptop and some jewelry had been taken, but the police apprehended the suspect and retrieved her belongings as he was leaving the neighborhood. Gavin and Danielle had just left the police department to identify the suspect. He'd cleaned her pool a month ago.

"Dani is a little shaken up, so I'm going to take her to my house, " Gavin said.

"No, you can bring her here," Donovan insisted.

"D, we are closer to my house. It makes more sense for her to stay with me, you know, at my house. We called your parents to let them know what happened."

Donovan smiled to himself. He knew that Gavin was very protective of Danielle. They had been dancing around their attraction to one another for years. "Okay. Gavin, let me speak to her."

Before he could speak, she said, "Donovan, I'm okay. I just need a hot bath and a pint of strawberry ice cream. We're closer to Gavin's. I'll call you in the morning. I love you." She disconnected the call.

Donovan was looking at the phone when Ms. Evelyn and Jade entered his office.

"Is Danielle okay?"

"Yes, she is fine." He told them about his conversation with Gavin and Danielle.

"Well, well, hmmm. I'm going back to play with the kids," Ms. Evelyn said as she left Donovan's office.

"What's going on between Gavin and Danielle? They're into each other, right?" Jade asked Donovan. "When did it start and how long have they pretended that it doesn't exist?"

"Mom thinks things changed between them after Danielle's

senior prom. Danielle's high school boyfriend broke up with her two weeks before. She was heartbroken and humiliated. Gavin and I came home from college to rough the guy up a bit. He hated to see Danielle so miserable and offered to take her to the prom. My mom was thankful and offered to pay for his tuxedo. He declined Mom's offer, saying that if he had a sister that I would do the same. Danielle hated the idea. She said everyone would think that Gavin was just taking her because she was my little sister. Gavin promised to make everything special, so Danielle agreed. He was a man of his word. The week of prom, Gavin sent something special to the school for Danielle each day. The gifts included flowers, balloons, teddy bears, and candy. By the end of the week, everyone at the school thought that they were a real couple. Mom said when Danielle walked down the stairs that night, she saw a spark of awareness in Gavin's eyes. And of course, to Danielle, Gavin was her knight in shining armor."

"So neither has ever said anything."

"No, never."

"It has to be frustrating for both of them."

"All Gavin has to do is admit his feelings and ask me."

"You're kidding, right? Ask what? They're both adults."

"Maybe, but she is my sister. He attempted to talk to her years ago, maybe two months after Danielle's prom. But it was around that time that his ex-girlfriend told him she was four months pregnant with Sydnee."

Jade's stomach dropped and she felt the color draining from her face.

Donovan immediately noticed the change in Jade's facial expression and asked, "Are you okay?"

"Yes, my stomach...I guess I ate too fast. What happened with Sydnee's mom? Where is she?"

"She and Gavin dated on and off through college. He'd loved her at one point, but they had moved on before she discovered that she was pregnant. She and Gavin both believed in doing the responsible thing and got married.

They were married for eight years before they both agreed to go their separate ways. They now share joint custody of Sydnee. She visits her mom during the holidays and summer months.

"After the divorce, Gavin and Sydnee moved back to Atlanta. Danielle moved back around the same time. Sydnee fell in love with Danielle and they soon became inseparable. Both Gavin and Danielle have dated other people, but their relationships would only go so far, as their hearts belonged to one another. Everyone has accused them of being more than 'friends'."

"Six years. That's crazy," Jade said.

"It is, but I think tonight has truly set the wheels in motion for them. There was something different in Gavin's voice... protectiveness and possessiveness," Donovan replied.

"I hope so."

"Me too, I want everyone to have what I have."

"And what is that?"

"Love, Ms. Jade, love," he said as he invaded her personal space and embraced her. He lowered his lips to her and made love to her mouth. Jade whimpered with pleasure.

Their moment was interrupted by Kamia knocking on the door.

"Daddy and Jade, hurry up."

Jade and Donovan laughed and said, "Coming."

Chapter Eighteen

It had been five days since Donovan and Jade made love. She wasn't comfortable with the idea of making love while everyone was in the house, or even sleeping in the same room with him. Each night after the children were asleep, she would retreat to his room until around midnight. They would watch TV or talk. She simply enjoyed the time and the closeness.

Tonight Donovan seemed totally preoccupied with his work. He usually stopped working when she came in the room, but tonight he didn't. Jade watched TV and tried to engage Donovan in conversation periodically.

"Natalie and Khalil are adjusting well. They're excited about the decorations we picked for their rooms. I just hope it all comes together and they like the space I create for them," Jade commented.

"Babe, they're fourteen and fifteen. It can't be that hard. And if nothing else, they think the world of you. Do you have everything you need to finish?"

"This is important to me. I want their rooms to be a place of security, where they can grow into themselves and start to believe in their dreams." There was a long pause. Jade sighed and then firmly said, "Donovan! Are you listening to me? "

Donovan looked up from his laptop and said, "Yes, babe, I hear you. Thanks for caring so much for my kids. It'll be fine. "

Jade was certain that he hadn't meant anything by the "my kids" comment, but she was hurt, nonetheless. His kids? She thought of them as their kids. She considered them a family. Disappointed, Jade got up from the bed and said, "I'm going to bed. Don't stay up too late. You promised to take Khalil driving in the morning, before taking him to shop for new school clothes."

"That's why I'm still awake. I am nervous as bananas about teaching Khalil to drive."

"You're nervous? What car are you going to use?" Jade asked curiously.

"I'll probably take the Cutlass," Donovan said, without looking up from the computer.

Jade looked at him in disbelief. Donovan was referring to his 1970 White Cutlass 442.

"Why would you teach him how to drive in that car? Isn't it a part of your collection? He'll be nervous," Jade stated and shook her head in disbelief.

"Yes, the Cutlass is a collector's dream, but it is just a car. Khalil's life is priceless and could never be replaced. I want him to learn to drive responsibly. The car is just that, a car." Donovan looked at Jade.

His logic pleased her.

Jade smiled at the man she had fallen in love with for a second time. She walked over to him and kissed him hard.

"Ms. Evelyn and I are taking the girls school shopping tomorrow for clothes and school supplies, too. I have a list for Khalil's supplies, so we'll pick those up as well."

"Okay, do I need to transfer money to the household account?"

"Yes. Ms. Evelyn and I were talking and we both agree that $2,500 should be enough."

"What? Why so much?"

"It's for three girls, one of whom is a teenager. The twins, Natalie, and Khalil have outgrown most of their clothing. We donated their clothes and shoes to Brenda's New Beginnings."

"What's that?" Donovan asked.

"It's a local shelter for women and children," she answered.

"Okay, that's great, babe. Did you or Ms. Evelyn order laptops for Natalie and Khalil?"

"Yes, they'll be delivered to your office on Thursday for your IT guy to set up. I also ordered a camcorder."

"A camcorder." Donovan looked up with a sly grin on his face. He pointed to himself and then to her. "For me and you."

Jade laughed and blushed, "You wish. No movie-making

here. D, it's for the kids' events."

"You can't blame me for trying." He pulled her to his lap and kissed her feverishly. His hand rubbed her gently, longing to touch her there. "I miss being inside of you."

Jade pulled away. She wanted Donovan so badly that she could taste him, but not tonight.

"I miss you, too. Would you like your door closed?" Jade asked as she began to leave.

"Yes, please."

*****

Donovan smiled as he looked up at Jade's retreating back. Only she could be that sexy dressed in cotton pink and green pajamas. She had purchased similar pajamas and socks for the girls. They all seemed to be coordinated day and night.

Unbeknownst to Jade, Donovan had been working on a proposal for Marshall Construction, regarding the renovation of Holly Gardens and the Community Center, since she first told him about it. He wanted to ensure that her project was successful. It was personal for Jade and that made it personal for him.

Periodically, Jade had mentioned the difficulties she was experiencing with getting the project funded. Several of her funding sources had backed out, and the city was holding up the building permits. He could tell that she was losing her fighting spirit.

Pearl provided Donovan with a copy of the contracts with the city, the construction agency, and the funding sources. Donovan smiled at the not-so-subtle way Pearl conveyed her message. "Donovan, make it happen for her sake and yours. I want my daughter to be happy, and right now you and these kids are her total source of happiness."

Although Donovan had an exemplary security system, he walked through the house to check the doors each night. He would look in on Jade and the kids. Jade left her door open in case the children needed her, and he usually went in to kiss her on the forehead. She would always stir and smile at him when he entered the room. She brought such joy to his life.

For the past several nights, when he checked on Jade, he was astonished to find she was not in the bed alone. The girls were in the bed with her. Jade had mentioned not sleeping well and he thought it was because she was anxious about finishing the decorations in the main house. He had no idea that she was sharing her bed with three girls. Although the bed was king-sized, it had to be uncomfortable with four bodies. He hadn't expected tonight to be any different, until he saw Khalil asleep on the chaise lounge chair in the room. He decided to move the twins back to their room, but left Natalie in the bed with Jade, as Jade had become a "security blanket" for her.

Jade made the family unit work. Initially, it appeared that Khalil and Natalie favored Jade, but that was understandable, as Jade was there when Donovan picked them up from the foster home. The twins naturally favored Ms. Evelyn, as she had raised them for four years. Jade made a conscious effort to help develop a relationship between Ms. Evelyn, Natalie, and Khalil without making the twins feel left out. She also reminded Donovan of his role in the family as father and provider. She didn't accept work excuses over his parenting responsibilities.

He loved her for loving him, in spite of what loving him required.

Chapter Nineteen

Early the following morning, Jade's cell phone chimed and vibrated, indicating that she had a text message. It was Monique, her assistant from Holly Health. Monique's regular work calls had increased from two times a month to weekly. Jade made it a point to check in with Monique, Cheryl, and Emanuel frequently.

A lot had happened in her life in just a matter of months. She hadn't worked since Nathan's death. She turned over many of her responsibilities to Teresa and Emanuel, with Monique now assisting them. She had also promoted one of the office managers to fill Monique's previous position and assist Monique.

A sting of guilt flashed throughout Jade's body as she thought about the Holly Gardens project; she needed to begin working on it again. No one else knew the ins and outs of the project like she did. The project was to symbolize a memorial to Jonothan for all his hard work and dedication to the community he grew up in and loved.

Jade got up quietly, hoping not to disturb the girls, who were still piled in her bed.

The text message read, "Good morning. I know you're up. Call me as soon as you can."

Jade made her way to the kitchen to start coffee. She dialed Monique's number.

"Good morning, Jade."

"Good morning, Monique. "

"Jade, you sound like you are glowing."

"I am!" she screamed. "Wait, does glowing really have a sound?"

"Yes, it does. Jade, are you glowing, as in *man glowing*?" Monique inquired.

"Yes. I am *man glowing*. I am in love," Jade responded.

"Yes, you are," Donovan whispered as he kissed Jade on

the back of her neck and tapped her buttocks.

Jade smiled and blushed as she was embarrassed; she did not hear him come into the kitchen. Her thoughts were interrupted by Monique's professional tone, "Jade, you have been gone for more than six months and everyone in the office has become nervous about their jobs. They are wondering what is going to happen with Holly Health and Community Services. Cheryl, Emanuel, and I have tried to reassure the staff and patients that all is well. You have been the face of Holly Health since Jonothan's death. They need to see you and know that you are okay."

Jade was surprised by Monique's comments. "I have spoken to one of you every week for the last six months and no one bothered to tell me about this before. Why haven't any of you mentioned this before?"

"Mainly because you sound amazing, like you're living again. We didn't want to bother you. But I can't pretend there isn't a problem. Teresa and Emanuel will be angry that I've called, but I thought you should know."

"Thank you, Monique. Let me talk with my family and I'll call you back with the date of my return."

Donovan prepared coffee for them both and then sat at the table reading the paper. He knew from what he'd overheard of Jade's conversation that something was up. But he waited for her to speak.

Jade sat next to Donovan and sipped her coffee. She was aware that he had heard her end of the conversation with Monique and was afraid to talk, afraid that once she started she wouldn't be able to stop. Now was not the time for her to tell Donovan everything. At least two minutes passed before she spoke.

"I'm sure you heard some, if not all of my conversation. That was Monique, my Executive Assistant; she has been assisting Teresa and Emanuel with managing my duties since my leave of absence from work."

Donovan was well informed about Jade's professional

achievements and obligations. But for the level of intimacy this moment symbolized for him and Jade, Donovan appeared clueless, just nodding to indicate that he was listening.

"Since my leave of absence in January, I've been working and monitoring things here and there, but not working as much as I should. My business partners, staff, patients, and community members are nervous about the future of Holly Health and the birth of Holly Gardens. I need to go…"

"I see, you need to go and do damage control," Donovan said. "You need to hold hands, soothe nerves, and calm the minds of your staff and the people you serve. I understand and I support you."

"I knew you would understand. It's the children I am worried about. School starts next week. I don't want to disrupt our routine."

"Jade, they'll be fine. Ms. Evelyn has everything under control."

"I know she does, but she has more people to take care of now and I wanted to help out as much as possible. What time are you and Khalil leaving to go driving?"

"7:30."

"It's 7:30 now. You both need to eat breakfast."

Khalil entered the room with a big smile on his face and said, "Good morning."

"We'll pick up breakfast after we finish with our lesson," Donovan said. "We're picking up Delshon at 11:00 and Gavin will meet us at the mall."

"But--" was all Jade could get out before Donovan kissed her on the cheek. Khalil followed suit, kissing her on the other cheek, and then they both were walking out the door. She followed and yelled, "Be safe, have fun and be back by five!"

Jade closed the door, smiled, and thought to herself, *The men in my life!*

Jade went back upstairs to shower and get dressed, hoping to have breakfast prepared before the girls woke up. They had to stay on schedule if today was going to be productive.

*****

Ms. Evelyn was standing at the stove preparing breakfast when Jade returned to the kitchen. She knew that they would need energy and patience if their day of shopping was to go well. Shopping with three teenagers and the twins, what had they been thinking? Ms. Evelyn shook her head and smiled.

"Good morning. What are you thinking about?" Jade asked as she entered the kitchen.

Ms. Evelyn chuckled, "Our shopping experience today. What were you thinking about?"

"Getting it over with! I guess."

Then they both laughed .

The sound of the doorbell rang throughout the house.

"That's probably Danielle and Sydnee. I'll be right back."

"Good morning, come on in," Jade greeted Danielle and Sydnee.

"Good morning," they responded.

"Sydnee, the girls are upstairs. Go on up."

Jade turned to Danielle, "You look tired. What's up?"

"I haven't had my coffee," Danielle responded, walking towards the kitchen.

"Good morning, Ms. Evelyn," Danielle said as she fixed a cup of coffee then took a seat at the island.

"Good morning. Have you and Sydnee eaten?" Ms. Evelyn asked Danielle.

"No, you cooked enough for us, right?"

"Yes, Dani," Ms. Evelyn said. "Please set the table with paper products. We don't have time to clean dishes. These pots are going in the dishwasher."

Jade and Danielle looked at Ms. Evelyn in surprise.

"Don't look at me like that. We have a lot of children coming and going through here. I am working smarter, not harder."

Jade sighed, "I have something I need to talk to you both about. I talked with Donovan early this morning."

"How early?" Danielle said in a sassy tone.

Jade nudged her and said, "Stop that."

"Go ahead, Jade; I'll be calling the girls down soon," Ms. Evelyn said.

"I need to go home for a while. I have to take care of some things regarding the community center. I've been gone too long."

Jade explained everything to Ms. Evelyn and Danielle. They both reassured her that all would be fine with the children. Ms. Evelyn thought that it would be best for Jade to tell the children after dinner tonight.

"Are you prepared to answer any questions they may have?"

"I guess. I hope."

"Is there a future for you and Donovan?" Ms. Evelyn continued. "Have you talked about how you'll make it all work?"

"I'd love for there to be, but we haven't talked about how to make it work."

"When are you leaving? How long will you be gone?"

"Well, I want to be here for the first week of school. So, I'm thinking of leaving the Saturday after school starts." She paused. "Honestly, I'm not sure how long I'll be gone. When I get there, I'll know all that needs to be done. I will call every evening as often as you or the children need me. This is so hard." Jade closed her eyes to stop the tears from falling.

Ms. Evelyn reached for her. "You've been talking about the children adjusting, but I'm more worried about you. Jade, it will all work out. God's timing is never off. It is our reactions to His timing that determine the productivity of our outcomes.

"Now, get your face straight while I call the girls down for breakfast. Girls, please come down for breakfast," Ms. Evelyn said through the intercom system.

She heard a chorus of "Yes, ma'am" and footsteps. Ms. Evelyn smiled, overwhelmed with an abundance of joy. The house was full of people and love.

*****

To say the least, the afternoon of shopping was very eventful, but a success. As planned, the family met back home around 5 p.m. so the children could show off and model their new attire. Khalil and Delshon also showed what they had purchased, but were totally against modeling.

On the other hand, the girls couldn't wait to show off their new clothes.

"All of that definitely looks like more than $2,500." Donovan smiled.

"We only spent $1,500," Jade said smartly.

"Okay, ladies and gentlemen, prepare to be entertained by our lovely models," Danielle said in her best commentator voice, before sitting next to Gavin on the loveseat.

Delshon started music and the girls took turns strutting through the family room. The twins walked in looking like an advertisement for The Gap.

"Natalie, Sydnee, and Lyric, you're up. Come on out," Jade yelled.

Natalie walked into the family room looking like a sophisticated teen girl. Everyone clapped their approval.

"Nat, you look great. I think that's my favorite," Danielle said.

"Lyric and Sydnee, lookin' good, ladies," Jade yelled.

"Dang, Nat, you wearin' that?" Delshon looked at Khalil and added, "Man, when did Lil' Sis grow up?"

Khalil responded, "Apparently today."

"Alright, kids, go change and meet us in the dining room for dinner. Danielle, I need your help," Ms. Evelyn said, ushering the kids out of the family room.

Gavin and Jade waited for Donovan to speak.

Donovan turned to Jade and spoke in a shocked voice. "How is it that Natalie goes from wearing basketball shorts and a T-shirt to being a model for some girly store? Were the clothes her choice or yours, Jade?"

"What! Are you serious?" Jade took a step back. She did

not like the accusatory tone Donovan was taking with her.

"Hey, wait, both of you." Gavin attempted to intervene.

"Donovan Jamal Johnson, get a clue. Natalie is fifteen and trying to find herself. I was just as surprised as you are by her selections. "

"Answer the question, Jade. Did you pick out these clothes?"

"No. Natalie picked out her own clothes. The clothes are appropriate, not low-cut or too tight. So what's the problem?"

"Jade, she looks totally different. The clothes and the makeup--well, that caught me off guard."

"Listen, you and Khalil are the male figures in Natalie's life. You both may not be ready for this change, but Natalie is. Now, I suggest you get it together and go tell your daughter how beautiful she is. Then you speak to Khalil. If she receives positive interaction from the males in her life at home, the attention that other boys give will not be as important. Boys are the least of your worries for now."

Jade rolled her eyes at both Donovan and Gavin.

Gavin threw up his hands. "For the record, I agree with Jade 100%."

"Talk to him," Jade said, walking away.

"Look, man, everything she said is on point. Natalie will look to you and Khalil for approval. You can and will have to learn to deal with the idea of boys in her life and the twins. So get over yourself and let's go eat," Gavin said before walking toward the kitchen.

He turned around, chuckled, and said, "Man, she is really angry. Good luck."

Donovan followed Jade's advice and told Natalie that he thought that she'd gotten nice things for school. He complimented her on how beautiful she was.

As if rehearsed, Gavin, Khalil, and Delshon complimented Natalie too.

Natalie hugged Donovan and whispered in his ear, "Thank you, what you think really matters to me."

Donovan's heart swelled with fatherly pride and he whispered back, "*I love you*, too."

He winked at Jade and she turned her head. Dang, he was in the doghouse.

After everyone finished eating, Jade asked for their attention.

"I have some news that I need to share with you. But first I want you all to know that I love you."

"Me too," Delshon said jokingly.

"You too, Delshon," Jade answered, and the tears began to form in her eyes. If she cried, the girls would cry. She closed her eyes, took a deep breath, and clenched her necklace in her hand. "I have to…"

"What?" the children asked.

Ms. Evelyn stood next to Jade and spoke for her. "Jade has to go home for a while. She has to take care of some things and check on people who depend on her."

"We depend on her!" Kamia yelled.

"We want you here with us." Kamill's voice was laced with sadness.

"Yes, Kamill, we all want Jade here, but she has responsibilities at home," Ms. Evelyn said.

Natalie's voice was low and trembling, "How long will you be gone?"

"I honestly don't know, but every minute I am away I will be missing all of you." Jade stepped next to Natalie and placed her hand on her arm. "I'll be back as soon as I can."

Donovan finally spoke up. "She'll call you, and you can call her anytime, right, Jade?"

"And text?" Khalil asked.

"Yes, of course. I'll visit on weekends, and don't forget Khalil's birthday is coming up. I can't miss that."

Jade noticed Kamia's blank expression. She added, "You can still sleep in my bed and pretend I'm there." The statement brought a smile to the child's face.

Lyric, Natalie's best friend, asked, "When are you leaving?"

"In two weeks."

"Cool. I thought you were going to say something like tomorrow."

Khalil took a deep breath and added, "Thanks for the heads-up."

Jade's heart melted. She would miss them so much.

"Group hug," Donovan said.

Everyone gathered around Jade. Kamia, Khalil, and Natalie were the closest to her. She looked up into Donovan's eyes and he mouthed the words, I love you. Jade nodded to keep the tears from falling.

Chapter Twenty

There were no words to express Donovan's gratitude for all that Jade had done for his family.

Once the redecoration and renovations to the main house were completed, the family moved back in and everything was perfect. The house was beautiful, beyond anything that he could have imagined. As a small token of appreciation, Donovan reserved Jade and himself a room at the Atlanta Evergreen Marriott Conference Resort in Stone Mountain for three nights. It had been a few weeks since they made love, and he missed her. He hoped that she would agree to spend this time with him before she returned home.

Jade eagerly accepted Donovan's invitation to go; it was one of her favorite places. The last time she had stayed there was shortly after Jonothan's death. The resort had beautiful property and had been the perfect getaway for her. She had hiked and spent time in the spa.

Grief and guilt tried to visit Jade, but she denied them access. She looked forward to sharing time with Donovan there. This time alone would be the perfect opportunity for Jade to tell Donovan of the things she had hidden in her secret place deep within. Yes, she would tell him everything.

Jade reached for the phone and called Onyx and Tia.

"Onyx and Tia, are you on the line?"

"I'm here," Onyx chimed in.

"I'm here," Tia answered.

"Donovan and I are going to Evergreen Resort for a few days. We leave tomorrow."

"That's nice," Onyx said, sounding distant.

Jade couldn't tell if it was the connection or a lack of feeling in her sister's voice.

"Yes, and I am looking forward to our time alone. I love him."

"Jade, that's been clear, but it is good to know that you've accepted it," Tia said sincerely.

"I think it's time to tell him," Jade said.

"Tell him what?" Tia asked.

"Everything."

"Everything Do you mean *everything*?" Onyx asked, sounding more alert and concerned.

"Yes, I have to."

"Why?" they both asked.

"I love him and I should have told him back then. I can't give him my all and not tell him."

"Jade, what if he can't forgive you?" Tia asked.

"He will forgive me. It will be hard at first, but he will."

"Jade, you're kidding, right! He will be so hurt. You can't believe that *love conquers* all applies here. You can't be that naïve," Onyx yelled.

"No, Onyx, I know it won't be easy. But I know that we haven't found each other simply to lose one another again. And yes, I still believe in love. The same kind of love you and I grew up witnessing."

"Whatever," Onyx's tone was frustrated.

"Onyx, what's going on with you?"

"Nothing, I just can't believe in the love Mom and Dad had, not right now! I can't believe in the melodies Chaka Khan, Anita Baker, and Teddy Pendergrass sang about anymore."

"What do you mean you can't believe in love, right now? See, Mom was right...that's why she flew back to Hawaii."

"What do you mean?" Onyx asked.

To prevent the conversation from escalating, Tia said, "Jade, this conversation is about you and Donovan. Just know that however this turns out, Onyx and I will be here for you."

"Jade!"

"Onyx, stop yelling." Tia intervened again.

"Onyx, Mom thinks you're hiding something from us. She said it was time to pull your skeletons out of the closet."

Onyx chuckled. "He is definitely not a skeleton. He is a living and breathing man."

"He?" echoed gasps from Tia and Jade, but both went silent. Onyx was never very open about her personal life.

"I met someone on vacation, before my promotion to Major this past December," Onyx went on. "He touched me to the very core and changed me. I was totally open and vulnerable when we were together. And there are times now when I still feel opened up. He branded me. I still crave his touch and I may never feel it again.

"So, you all are right, I am different. I am a Major in the United States Army. My profession dictates that it is dangerous for me to care or feel, yet I yearn to feel this man close to me at all times. "

"Onyx, I'm sorry," Jade said.

"Don't be. I fell in love and I walked away from it. No more about me."

"Onyx," Tia said.

"No." Onyx took a deep breath, then replied, "This conversation is over. Back to you and Donovan, Jade. He will forgive you over time, but his initial response will be anger and sadness. It's not going to be nice."

"Onyx, I was there to witness the love they shared in college and I have been privy to observe the love they share now. He loves you, Jade, but he will be hurt," Tia agreed.

"Jade, whatever happens, we'll be here to help you through it," Onyx replied.

"Thank you and I love you both," Jade said.

"Love you more," Tia and Onyx said as they all disconnected the call.

Onyx looked in the mirror at her reflection and placed her hand over her heart. He had definitely branded her. She reached for her phone and searched through her playlist for the ole'-school classics that her parents jammed to, like Chaka Khan's "Sweet Thang" or "Do You Love Me Still", Anita Baker's "Sweet Love", and Teddy Pendergrass's "If You Don't Know Me by Now."

Chapter Twenty-One

Donovan and Jade were in their suite at the resort discussing their dinner plans when her cell phone buzzed.

"Honey, I thought we agreed to no cell phones while we are here," Donovan said. "Ms. Evelyn and your mom have the hotel's number in case of an emergency. Will you please turn off your cell phone?"

To Donovan's amazement, she gave him the phone without an argument.

She walked out onto the balcony and marveled at the view of the mountain while Donovan marveled at the sight of her. She was wearing a light blue sundress that accentuated every new curve of her body and gave a glimpse of her ample breasts.

Donovan walked out onto the balcony and embraced Jade from behind. She snuggled close to him. He sighed at the perfect fit of her body against his and inhaled her scent. Her perfume and natural pheromones heightened his senses.

"It's a beautiful day," Jade said in a sing-song tone.

"Not as beautiful as you," he whispered in her ear.

Jade rubbed her body against his and Donovan couldn't restrain himself. He guided Jade back inside of their suite. He wrapped his arm around her waist, led her to the bed and laid her down on her stomach. He pressed and rubbed his hard body against her. His desire for her was evident.

Jade moaned Donovan's name as she lifted her hips, a non-verbal command for him. She turned her head and body to look at him. His eyes held her in a gaze and he kissed her. Their tongues danced to a melody that only they could hear.

As if on cue, he used one hand to caress her hip and the other to raise her dress. He lifted his body to unzip his shorts and reached in to release his hard penis. When his penis made contact with Jade's skin, she moaned at the feel of its heat. She wiggled and opened her legs to allow him access. He could smell her essence, evidence of her desire for him. He slid her lacy panties to the side.

In one slow, sensual thrust, Donovan filled her and they both moaned in satisfaction. He didn't move to allow time for Jade's body to adjust to him and to avoid losing control over his own body. She was tight and sheathed him like a glove. Donovan whispered sensual words in Jade's ear, nibbled on her earlobe, and kissed the back of her neck.

As if second nature, her body responded. Jade repositioned herself, with her face down and her hips up. She began speaking passionately as she moved her body. "I missed you being inside of me. Ummm... Donovan, love me deeper, love me harder. I want more... love me, love me..." Her words turned into low moans and panting that filled the room. She pushed back onto Donovan, clenched her muscles and established a rhythm. Her body began to spiral from the intensity of their lovemaking.

Donovan loved the way she felt as she pushed back on what she knew was hers alone. With his simple gestures of light taps on her left hip and two hard thrusts, Donovan compelled Jade to surrender for the ride. He reached up and intertwined his fingers with hers. He enjoyed the sound of Jade saying his name over and over with each of his deep strokes and without warning, he exploded into orgasmic ecstasy.

Donovan and Jade spent the remainder of the evening in their suite. They made long slow love, napped, showered, and ordered dinner. After sharing dinner, Jade needed to talk. She wanted to tell Donovan about Jonothan.

"Donovan, I want to talk about Jonothan, the accident, and my baby."

"Okay, would you like to sit out on the balcony?"

"Yes," Jade said.

Donovan and Jade settled themselves side by side on the balcony of their suite.

"I know sharing this isn't easy, but I'm glad you trust me enough to do it."

"It's time that you know everything. After our relationship ended, I didn't have a desire to date or entertain the thought of loving another man. Jonothan pursued me anyway, courted me, and after two years I fell hopelessly in love with him. We shared a loving marriage and a successful business for eight years. Three years ago, Jonothan and I were on our way home from having dinner with his parents when we were hit by a drunk driver. The impact of the car caused our SUV to spin and flip. Jonothan was ejected from the car.

He was wearing a seatbelt, but it malfunctioned. I was eight months pregnant, and the physical trauma caused the miscarriage of our daughter. Her name would have been Amber. I returned to work only two weeks after the accident. I started working on the Holly Gardens expansion project as a memorial to Jonothan. I buried myself in the work to avoid the feelings and to deal with the losses I'd experienced. I've been stuck in my grieving process for the past three years. If Tia and Onyx hadn't set up our meeting again, I would still be stuck. I feel so blessed to have you in my life, again. But there is something else that I need to tell you."

"Shh, Jade, listen to me. Jade, you are more than enough for me. Thank you for giving us a second chance. Thank you for accepting me and the children. *We are blessed to have you.*" Donovan stood and took Jade by the hand and they walked back inside.

"I need you to hold me," she said, as the tears slowly fell from her eyes and she tucked the sadness back into her heart. She prayed for strength to tell Donovan more tomorrow.

Donovan gathered Jade close to him.

"It's okay, baby, I'm here. I love you."

"I love you, too."

They snuggled close until they both fell asleep.

*****

Jade and Donovan couldn't have asked for more, their time at the resort had been wonderful. They made love numerous times in various positions. They walked the nature preservation trail and attempted rock climbing. Jade's day at the spa was relaxing and rejuvenating.

On the last night at the resort, they agreed to have dinner in their suite. Jade became overwhelmed with emotions. She was in love with Donovan and wanted to give herself to him completely. She had to tell him everything now. She only prayed that he would understand.

"Donovan, there is something else that I need to tell you. Please come here and sit with me."

Donovan sat next to Jade and automatically reached for her hand. "Babe, what's wrong? You're shaking."

"Donovan, please let me speak. I've held this long enough. So, please listen. Donovan, I...oh God." Jade took a deep breath and continued. "A month after we broke up in college, I found out that I was pregnant." Jade reached deep within the secret place that held the painful memories and tears began to flow from her eyes.

She heard Donovan blow out several sharp breaths. He stood up and walked to the balcony, and Jade followed as she continued speaking.

"You had already left for your internship with Sims Financial Corporation. I'd planned to tell you when you came back, but by that time I had miscarried our baby girl... Diamond. I wanted to name her Diamond."

Jade couldn't look at him, but she heard his rapid breathing and knew that he was angry.

"When you returned, I saw you and Asia together and you seemed happy. I didn't want to cause you any pain and I wasn't sure how you would respond. So I didn't tell you about her."

"You chose not to tell me, about my baby....our baby. How could you?" Donovan took several deep breaths in an attempt to gain control of his emotions and his voice. "You should have told me everything! I could have been there for you. We could have been there for each other. You had no right to keep this from me. I knew something was wrong, when I came to the apartment to see you that day. I knew something was wrong. And for the record, we did not break up: YOU LEFT ME!"

"I'm sorry. At the time, I thought it was best. Now I know different. I love you and I want to share my life with you. I know you're angry, but we can work through this together. Donovan, please, please forgive me."

"That's what you were trying to tell me that night at Skipper's....Diamond...she was real, our baby."

As Jade took steps toward Donovan, he moved back and held his hand up.

"Please!" Jade yelled.

He closed his eyes and said, "Don't touch me. I--I don't know--I need some time."

"Well, I'll leave earlier than we planned, but I will not miss the kids' first day of school."

"No, you will miss their first day of school, because I am making your flight arrangements for tomorrow evening."

"Donovan, please...you can't."

"Watch me!" he yelled, leaving the hotel suite.

Jade stepped back and watched the man she loved walk out the door.

*****

When Donovan finally returned to the hotel room, he said, "Pack your things; we are leaving."

He felt like he couldn't breathe. Jade had been pregnant with his child, a daughter, miscarried, and didn't tell him until now, fourteen years later. How in the hell was he supposed to deal with this and the fact that she'd lied to him for all these months?

The ride home was almost unbearable for Jade. Donovan was angry beyond measure and rightfully so. She had been young, afraid, and hadn't chosen wisely. Now, she had to suffer the consequences of her actions. Donovan would need time to grieve the loss of their daughter, just as she had to fourteen years ago. She'd hoped that they could work through the process together, but now she was sure that was not an option.

Once they returned to the house, Jade decided that it would be best for her to leave Donovan's home that night. She talked with Ms. Evelyn and the children about leaving and promised to call every night and visit when she could. Then she called Tia to ask her to pick her up.

Jade entered Donovan's office and found him looking out the window. With his back to her, she said, "You don't have to arrange my flight. Tia's here to pick me up."

Donovan remained silent and continued to gaze out of the window.

"I love you," Jade said in a whisper as the tears filled her eyes.

He turned slightly, only to see her retreating back. His mind was consumed with "What ifs?," "Whens?," "Whys?," and "Hows?"

He and Jade had both believed in non-negotiable safe sex practices during their relationship. They had always protected one another. So how did she get pregnant? A haunting laugh escaped Donovan's lips. He and Jade were among the three percent that the warning labels represented.

Donovan had to process his emotions, but he had no idea how to start. Why would Jade keep this from him? Had she despised him that much or was she trying to spare him the pain?

Ms. Evelyn watched Jade leave the house in tears and safely get into Tia's car. She did not know what was going on, but she knew who did. "Donovan Jamal Johnson, what is going on?" Ms. Evelyn asked in a stern voice.

"Ma, not now, please," Donovan replied, never turning his chair to face Ms. Evelyn.

The tone of his voice had Ms. Evelyn rounding the desk and standing in front of him in seconds.

"Son, what is it?"

"Ma," was all he could get out, before his grief and pain overtook him.

Ms. Evelyn wrapped her arms around Donovan and he cried.

Chapter Twenty-Two

It had been a month since Jade left Atlanta, but it felt like a lifetime. She was sad and alone as she sat in her favorite room of the house. The room was a perfect reflection of her personality and style. The color palette was café au latte, sage, and antique gold with accents of lavender. Her frog fountain played a watery melody and vanilla, sage, and cinnamon-scented candles could be smelled throughout the room. Jade usually could find comfort and peace in this special room, but not today. Tears flowed down her cheeks. She missed Donovan and the children. She needed them as much as she needed her next breath.

As if on cue, Jade's cell phone buzzed, indicating a text message from Khalil. She smiled at the message:

"Thank you for the tutor. She is great and pretty! C-ya this weekend."

"You're welcome. I can't wait to see you," Jade texted back.

Jade wiped her tears and cleared her throat as she called the house.

Ms. Evelyn picked up. "Hi, what a pleasant surprise. You are calling early today."

"I know, but...."

"What is it, sweetie?"

"I miss all of you so much. Donovan still hasn't answered or responded to any of my calls or emails. I don't know what to think."

"He loves you, he's just hurt. Donovan deals with pain, loss, and disappointment differently. Normally, he suppresses his emotions and consumes himself with work. Right now, that isn't working. So he is forced to deal with his emotions and has no idea how to begin. I know that it's not an excuse, nor does it ease your pain."

"I know. I just wish I could..."

"Well you can't; healing takes time. You and Donovan both

have *let me fix it* personalities, but you both need to remember that God has all control and He doesn't make mistakes. Now let's talk about the girls' and Khalil's party this weekend."

Jade enjoyed her conversations with Ms. Evelyn and the children. Today was not an exception, until Ms. Evelyn told her that Donovan had started working later and later.

"He should be home with the children!" she yelled to no one but herself.

Jade called Donovan's personal cell, but it went straight to voicemail. She decided to call him in the office. The receptionist said he was meeting with Amelia and requested not to be disturbed.

Amelia and Donovan had been spending a lot of time together lately. Jade's mind raced with thoughts of him and Amelia. Feeling as if her heart had fallen into her gut, she ran to the bathroom and emptied the contents of her stomach.

*****

Although Donovan had told Ms. Evelyn that he wouldn't be home until 8 p.m., he decided to leave work early. He hadn't accomplished much, as his mind was on his family and Jade.

Now he was working long hours to avoid thinking of Jade, but working late had created another problem in his life. He'd left the majority of parenting up to Ms. Evelyn and his mom. Donovan shook his head and chastised himself. He was now the father of four beautiful and healthy children. He needed to be home more and active in the children's day-to-day lives.

Donovan needed to make several adjustments in his life. First, he needed to have a family meeting tonight. Secondly, he needed to change his work schedule. Although he was the CEO of Johnson and Johnson, LLC he had competent staff members who were just as invested in the success of the company. He would need to reorganize and reallocate the work load among his associates. Lastly, he needed to come to some type of mutual understanding with Jade. He knew that she called the children and Ms. Evelyn every day. He knew that she called his mom and sister weekly. He knew that she'd called him several times. He just didn't know how to move forward from the hurt and betrayal.

He shook his head once again, as if to physically remove Jade from his thoughts. He transitioned his thoughts to the children. Having Natalie and Khalil had been great for Kamia and Kamill, who were blossoming more and more. Kamia was no longer shy and reserved. She was more talkative and outgoing and her speech had improved significantly. Kamill was more relaxed. She hadn't had any dreams in months.

Natalie and Khalil had adjusted well to their new school. Khalil had been placed in Advanced English, Science, and Math classes. Advanced English was a challenge for Khalil, but he appeared to be studying more and asking for help when he needed it. He made the basketball team too. The coach was impressed with his gift for the sport. To eliminate arguing over the phone, Donovan had an additional phone line installed for Khalil and Natalie's calls. The ring tones for the two home phones were different.

Natalie was doing well academically and socially, too. She'd become a social butterfly and had also made the basketball team. Donovan was still having a difficult time with boys calling Natalie. The first time a boy called for her, Donovan told him that Natalie was not dating until she was twenty-one and hung up the phone. Ms. Evelyn intervened immediately, but Donovan refused to hear their logic until he had a conversation with Gavin.

"D, it's better to have an idea of who she is talking to. You have to be sensible. You can screen and monitor her calls from time to time. You have several daughters and it is not going to get easier. You have to be smarter and be at least twelve steps ahead of them."

Donovan agreed that Natalie deserved to be treated like the responsible teen she was. He began to allow Natalie to talk to boys, but on the house phone only. Boys were not to call her cell phone. If they did, she would lose her cell phone privileges for two months. He trusted Natalie. It was the boys he did not trust.

That night, Donovan arrived home in a record forty minutes. He noticed a late model two-door Honda Accord in the circular driveway, but it wasn't uncommon for Khalil or Natalie to have a friend over.

Donovan entered the kitchen to the scent of mouth-watering aromas. Ms. Evelyn and Natalie were cutting fresh vegetables at the kitchen island. He greeted the ladies in his life with a kiss on the forehead and silently wished that Jade was there. The twins were at the kitchen table completing their homework. Before leaving to put his briefcase in the home office, he asked, "Where is Khalil?"

Natalie looked to Ms. Evelyn, but neither responded to his question. Donovan wondered why they both looked like deer caught in headlights. He moved closer to Ms. Evelyn and asked the question again.

Ms. Evelyn put the knife down on the counter and wiped her hands on her apron.

"Khalil is in the dining room with Nyla, his tutor. The DJ is in the basement working on music for Saturday."

"What tutor and what DJ?

"Nyla started two weeks ago. You usually arrive home after she has left. The DJ is Khalil's friend, so they are working on music for the party together. Since you have not been available, I consulted Jade regarding the children's needs. I didn't think you would mind. She also sent you an email with all of the details," Ms. Evelyn said.

The last statement caught Donovan by surprise. It was like a punch to his gut. "Why would Jade feel comfortable enough to make decisions about my children without calling me first? Sending me an email with all of the details was not enough, if I didn't approve it," Donovan mumbled.

He knew Jade had tried to contact him, but he ignored her calls, her voice messages, and her text messages. He thought that it would be easier not to communicate with her. It was clear that she was not calling to talk about their relationship or to apologize, but was calling about Khalil, and that bothered him. Was she as miserable as he was by the conflict that existed between them? Was she miserable without him? It appeared as if all she cared about was the children.

Natalie interjected. "Jade did call, a lot. But you were either out or in your office," she said pointedly

Ms. Evelyn chastised Natalie with her eyes. She sensed that Donovan was annoyed and motioned for him to follow her into his office. They needed to have this "grown folk conversation" without little listening ears.

"Donovan, you haven't been the same since Jade left. Now you're spending a lot of time with Amelia. You have to understand that the children have a relationship with Jade. They love her and she loves them. Khalil confided in her about his difficulties with Advanced Placement English. She tried to call you on your cell phone, your office, and at the house, but you refused to respond."

"Things are complicated between us," Donovan said. "We both need time apart."

"Khalil needed help with English and Jade made sure that he got the assistance he needed! Nyla is a student at Spelman College and she is great with him. Khalil's grades and confidence have improved significantly. Don't question Jade's concern for Khalil. This is about his needs and not your ego. Okay? I've said enough. I suggest you call Jade from the house phone. She will answer. She'll think it is me or the kids because you're usually not home this early." Ms. Evelyn turned and walked out the door, closing it behind her.

Frustrated, Donovan picked up the house phone and called Jade on her home number.

"Hello."

"Hi, Jade."

Complete silence.

"Jade, I'm calling about the tutor you hired for Khalil and

the party you planned for him without my consent. You are spending my money like it's yours."

Complete silence.

"And you insult me by not getting the final approval from me, when it involves one of my children. Your behavior is unacceptable. I am upset with Ms. Evelyn, too. She should have never done anything without speaking to me first."

He heard a sharp intake of breath and knew that he had struck a nerve with Jade. He wasn't surprised when Jade hung up the phone, or when his cell phone rang two minutes later. In fact, he knew that the wrath was coming.

He answered the phone on the first ring, but didn't have to say a word. Jade's immediate verbal attack was panther-like.

"Donovan Jamal Johnson, don't you dare call me with your insults. Your behavior is unacceptable! You have four children who need you to be a full-time parent. Not a part-time parent. I called you the first night Khalil confided in me, but you were in a meeting. It appears that when you should be home, you are working. I called your office, your business cell, your personal cell, and the house. I left you several voicemails and sent a fax and an email. So, yes, I emailed you with the details, because if nothing else, you are a businessman. Check your Blackberry!

"Let's be clear, Khalil is the priority. He is a strong and intelligent young man; for him to reach out to me for assistance took courage.

"Since you were not available, I discussed everything with your mom and Ms. Evelyn. I care about the well-being of all the children. Nyla is a phenomenal person. She is the great-granddaughter of one of my granny's friends. I trust her and she has been a great tutor for Khalil. His grades have improved in the past two weeks.

"By the way, if I've offended you by spending *your* money without *your* consent…I DON'T apologize. The money spent was well worth it. I know and you know there is no amount of money you would not spend on your children when they need it or deserved it. So get over it! But we both know that money is not the real issue here."

Jade finally took a deep breath and resumed speaking.

"Look around, Donovan. You have a house full of beautiful and gifted children who love you. They should be your only priority now. Work and other personal relationships, specifically Amelia, should not be your priority. You have employees who are capable of running Johnson and Johnson. You need to get it together and keep it together for our family. I'm coming for Khalil's birthday party. We need to at least be cordial for the children's sake. Good night."

Click.

Donovan figured Jade was right in saying he was not being a full-time parent. He had missed so much. He also heard her when she'd said "our family." He realized that he would have to explain his relationship with Amelia soon.

Donovan left his office and headed to the dining room. He stood outside the door and listened as Nyla and Khalil interacted. Nyla challenged Khalil in a manner that sparked his curiosity.

Their tutoring session was ending when Donovan walked in and introduced himself. He invited Nyla to stay for dinner, but she declined. Ms. Evelyn insisted Nyla call when she arrived at her apartment, and then she and Donovan walked her out to her car and watched as she drove away.

"Jade's coming Friday."

"Yes, I know." Ms. Evelyn's tone was matter-of-fact.

"When were you going to tell me?"

"I knew she would. Maybe you should..."

"No, Ma," Donovan said.

She responded tenderly, "Okay, son. This *time* I won't push."

Donovan moved close and kissed her on the check.

"Thank you. Is there anything I can do to help with the party?"

"I may need you to run some errands on Friday."

"No problem. When is Khalil's next tutoring session?"

"Thursday, why?" she asked.

"Nyla needs new tires, and from the sound of the car, she may need some repairs. I'll schedule for the mechanic to pick up the car on Thursday. She can drive the Ford Edge until her car is repaired."

Donovan ensured the mechanic was there on Thursday to pick up Nyla's car. Before the tutoring session, Donovan explained to Nyla that he was concerned about her safety and would pay to have the car serviced.

Nyla cried and thanked Donovan for his generosity.

Later, she called and told Jade about Donovan's unselfish act and Jade was pleased. Although they were still at odds, she acknowledged that he was a kind and generous man.

Chapter Twenty-Three

J ade arrived Friday morning around 9 a.m., shortly after the kids left for school. She drove her car directly to the guest house, hoping to avoid passing Donovan as he left for work.

She was surprised to find Donovan asleep in the guest house's family room. He was gorgeous and still took her breath away. He was dressed in a pair of Eddie Bauer khaki shorts and a dill-colored Eddie Bauer T-shirt that complemented his complexion. He was dressed for comfort, but would easily turn the heads of many women.

Donovan woke with a start. The hairs on the back of his neck stood up and his penis hardened in response to her scent.

Donovan took a deep breath, turned his head, and met Jade's gaze.

"I thought you were arriving at eleven. You're early."

"No, actually I am on time. Where is Ms. Evelyn? Why aren't you at work?"

"She is at the main house. She sent me to double check the house and make sure you have everything you needed."

"Well that was thoughtful of her, but I've been talking with her throughout the morning," Jade said.

"Oh, oh … I see."

Jade's gaze moved from his eyes and settled on the hardness in his pants. Jade should have been more concerned about working towards their emotional reconciliation, but the physical attraction between her and Donovan was a distraction. She thought about doing things to Donovan that made her blush. She smiled at that side of her, the side that only she and Donovan were familiar with, as she stepped closer to him. She immediately felt his manhood and her body stirred with anticipation.

Donovan looked away, but Jade leaned forward and turned his face back to her. She used her other hand to reach down and massage his hardness.

In spite of himself, Donovan moaned with pleasure. "What are you doing? Step back."

"No," Jade said, kneeling before him as she unbuckled his shorts. "Come on, baby, help me. Lift up a little. I want to taste you."

Donovan complied. Jade maneuvered his shorts down to his ankles.

"Take them off," he demanded.

Jade removed his shoes and shorts while kissing and licking Donovan's thighs. She worked her way up and consumed her chocolate cone, from tip to base.

Donovan gripped the back of Jade's head, ready to satisfy her hunger. This turned Jade on to the maximum degree. She took him deep into her mouth. His sweet low moan of approval inspired Jade to use her tongue and mouth to bring Donovan to the edge of eruption, only to withdraw him from her mouth.

She stood and undressed before him. Donovan grew thicker and harder as her scent filled the room.

Jade mounted him, sliding down his length until he filled her. She clinched and released her vaginal muscles before she started a slow and thorough ride. She unhooked the clasp on the front of her bra to release her breasts. Donovan feasted on them while his hands roamed all over her body, pushing and pulling. He was not a breast man, a butt man, a thigh man, or a leg man. He was a Jade man. Everything about her turned him on. He held her hips as she rode him. When he felt her pace increase, his head began spinning and he rested it on her chest.

Jade slid down Donovan's shaft one last time before lifting his head and kissing him deeply. She released the kiss, and with Donovan still deep inside her, she turned her body, her back facing him. She reached down, grabbed her ankles, and rode Donovan until he said her name over and over.

The sound of her name on his lips brought Donovan back to reality. He would not allow her to dominate him this way.

Donovan counted to ten and then stood up, still connected to Jade. He positioned her on her knees to allow himself full access. He thrust hard in and out of her body.

Jade gripped the sofa and moaned. She glanced back at Donovan. "Baby, it's yours, please."

She tried to adjust her body, but Donovan thrust harder and deeper, and increased the pace. He made love to Jade with all the love, anger, and sadness he held in his heart. Jade had known that this love session would be different, but she never expected this.

He tapped her on her left buttock and right buttock and thrust deeper. In a low, but demanding tone, he spoke, "Tell me."

"Donovan..." she panted in between the thrusts and the taps, "...this is ...oh yes...it's yours...I'm yours, always."

He needed to see her face. Donovan picked her up and carried her to the bedroom, depositing her in the center of the bed.

Jade lay there waiting for Donovan to finish what she'd started. He grabbed her by the ankles, pulled her to the edge of the bed, and spread her legs apart. Her scent flooded his nostrils as he looked at her most intimate part and licked his lips in anticipation. He made love to her with his tongue and fingers until she was on the brink of orgasm.

Then he slid his body up her length, supporting his weight on his arms. He looked into her eyes as he entered her in one fast and powerful stroke. He moved deeper, increasing the intensity of each thrust. His eyes dared Jade to look away or break his gaze. When he saw pleasure and pain in her eyes, he slowed and softened his strokes, but Jade urged him on.

"No, baby, please, give it all to me. I want it all," she said, panting. She pushed against his body and clenched her muscles.

Donovan complied and made love to her hard until they both spiraled in ecstasy.

Both still panting, Donovan carried Jade to the bathroom.

He bathed her and she him, but no words were spoken. After drying themselves off, he carried Jade to the bed and gathered her close.

"We'll get back up this afternoon around noon. I don't want to talk, but I'm not ready to let you go. Ms. Evelyn knows we're here. She'll call when she needs us."

"Okay, but we have to talk at some point," Jade said apprehensively and snuggled closer to Donovan.

Donovan and Jade woke up later that afternoon around 1 p.m. They both dressed in silence, until he finally spoke. "I'm still working through everything. No question that I love you, but I haven't forgiven you. I know what happened today may have complicated things but, that was not my intention."

Jade was bothered by Donovan's comment. "I love you, wanted you---needed you, as much as you needed me. There is nothing complicated about that."

*****

Donovan and Jade spent the remainder of the day running last-minute errands for Khalil's birthday party. By late afternoon, everything was done. After returning from dinner with Donovan, the children, and Ms. Evelyn, Jade sat on the sofa in the guest house, reflecting on the events of the day, she smiled. It had been an unusual but pleasant day. Her heart was overflowing with joy from catching up with the children.

She and Khalil were walking through the garden when he said, "Thanks for everything."

"Of course it's not every day that one of my favorite guys turns sixteen. How many of your friends did you invite to the pool party?" Jade asked.

"Twenty, but only four are staying the night, everybody else will be family.

Nana Pearl called me today," he told Jade. "She wished me an early happy birthday. She said I'll be too busy to talk tomorrow, but she'd still text me. She said something about Auntie Onyx doing better, so she'll be back to visit us soon."

Jade was totally amused by what Khalil had said. When did the children start calling Onyx, Auntie? What else had she missed?

"How is Mia?" Jade asked.

"She's ok; the distance is hard. She'll be here tomorrow. She's been annoyed with me and about all the attention girls are giving me at school."

"Does she have a reason to be annoyed?"

"No."

"Really?"

"Yes, really. My heart is with her. Look, see for yourself."

He handed Jade a pink jewelry box. She opened it and to her surprise there was a sterling silver necklace with a heart-shaped lock and key charm.

"It's nice isn't it? Me and Uncle D picked it out."

"Yes, it is."

Jade smiled and returned the box to Khalil.

"I plan to give it to her tomorrow. Do you think she'll like it?"

"Yes, it's very pretty."

"Giving her this is major for me. Do you think that she'll understand?"

"She may. I know saying 'I Love You' with a gift or even saying the words is major. Are you prepared to say the words, in case she doesn't understand what the gift represents?"

"Yeah."

"Wow. How did you get so wise at fifteen?"

Khalil blushed, but answered with confidence, "Sixteen tomorrow, and don't forget handsome. Wise and handsome, that's me."

They both laughed.

Then Jade's thoughts transitioned to Donovan. She took a deep breath and moaned sensually. Their love session had been intense and phenomenal, but there was an awkwardness in their interactions with one another throughout the day. Although they both made a conscious effort to decrease the tension between them. They were polite and attentive to one another, but it only made their interactions appear manufactured and insincere.

Love and trust were essential components in any relationship. He hadn't forgiven her for not telling him about Diamond and she would have to regain his trust. She could see the pain and anguish in his eyes. He still needed time to grieve, heal, and forgive. After this visit, she would give him that time.

Jade tore herself from her thoughts; tomorrow would be a long day and she needed to get some sleep. After a long shower and applying a generous amount of orange blossom and honey body butter to her skin, she felt relaxed. She kneeled by her bed and prayed for her family, for Donovan, and for herself.

When she rose to her feet, she stared into the eyes of her man. Jade should have been startled because she did not hear him come in, but she wasn't. Donovan climbed into the bed and she did the same.

"You smell good."

"Thank you."

He pulled her close. Jade laid her head on his chest, and they slept. No other words were exchanged.

*****

The following evening…

Everyone had arrived and the party was in full swing by five o'clock. The kids were entertaining themselves in the pool. Daniel, Donovan, and Gavin were on full alert while they monitored the boys' interactions with the girls.

"I think it's time to eat," Daniel said.

"We'll eat when the kids are ready, gentlemen, go in the house, please," Ms. Evelyn said in a non-negotiable tone.

When the men were in the house, the women laughed so hard that tears came to their eyes.

"Sharron, I thought they were going to strike out. If looks could kill, those poor boys would be dead," Ms. Evelyn laughed.

"Dead. Dead. Dead. Those poor boys can't help themselves," Sharron responded.

"Not one time did they say anything about Khalil and Mia sharing the hammock," Danielle said.

"No, but I did. You see they're up sitting together by the pool," Sharron said.

Jade noticed that Mia was wearing the necklace that Khalil had purchased. He'd given it to her early. Jade smiled. He was definitely a smart young man.

Donovan was overwhelmed with loss and betrayal. Jade's visit and their last sexual encounter had only complicated things. He couldn't eat or sleep. He wanted the pain to go away, but didn't know what to do.

Donovan had escaped to his office and when he looked up he saw his parents standing in the doorway.

"Donovan, what's going on? Ms. Evelyn is worried about you. Now that I see you, so am I. What's going on between you and Jade?"

Donovan looked up at his mother with no words. His eyes filled with tears and she wrapped her arms around him. When he found the strength, he said, "Mom, when Jade broke up with me in college, she was two months pregnant. She miscarried at four months. How could she have kept that from me? The pregnancy and the miscarriage. How could she? She was alone and I should have been there for her. How could I not have known she was pregnant? Why didn't I know? I love her but I don't know what to do with this pain."

"If you love her, forgive her and work through the pain together."

"It's not that easy." Donovan sobbed.

"If you love her, both of you must work through this pain together," his father said as he moved into the room. "We've talked to Jade and she is in as much pain as you. She loves everything about you."

Sharron took a deep breath and sighed before speaking. "Now, let's talk."

"Mom please, not now."

"Yes, now! Through all our obstacles, look at the love your father and I share. It was worth it; he is the light of my world. You have the same light with Jade. Don't wait until it's too late." Sharron kissed her son on the cheek.

"Daniel, please talk some sense into your son. I am going back to my grandson's birthday party."

Donovan knew his mother's words were true, yet he didn't know how his heart would heal from this. But he knew that it would surely stop beating if he couldn't love Jade and have her in his life.

Daniel didn't talk. He listened as his son talked himself into a state of peace and resolution. He smiled inwardly, knowing love always prevailed.

*****

Everyone enjoyed the evening. By 9 p.m., Donovan's parents, Danielle, Amelia, Mia, and Gavin had already left. Lyric, Tia, and Sydnee were staying the night. When the girls were settled upstairs, Donovan went downstairs to remind the boys of the house rules.

Ms. Evelyn and Jade sat at the kitchen island, relieved that the evening was a success and that it was over.

"Appearances can be deceitful, so, tell me the truth," Ms. Evelyn said. "How are things between you and Donovan?"

"He hasn't forgiven me, but he came to me last night."

"Jade, you're too close for him not to come to you. But don't let that confuse you. He still needs time to heal, real time."

"I know, but I don't want to lose him."

"You won't. He'll forgive you, but he has to work through this in his own way."

"Yeah, but what does that mean?"

"His own way is whatever gives him peace. What helped

you find your peace? Have you really talked to Donovan about the pregnancy, about the miscarriage? Have you talked about all the hows and whys?"

"No, ma'am."

"Well honey, that's a good place to start. When he comes to you tonight, talk to him."

Donovan appeared at the door entrance.

"I want to thank both of you for making this a great day for Khalil. Good night." Donovan kissed Ms. Evelyn on the cheek, touched Jade on the arm, and went upstairs.

Jade leaned over and kissed Ms. Evelyn on the other cheek. "I'll see you in the morning. We have an army to cook breakfast for. Good night."

Ms. Evelyn reached for Jade's hand and said, "Jade, it will be fine. I'll watch you until you get to the guest house."

*****

Donovan watched Jade from his bedroom window. Each of her steps seemed labored. The stress between them was taking a toll on them both.

He took a long, hot shower and climbed into bed. Sleep didn't come, as he was unable to clear his mind of Jade. She was so close yet so far from him. The pull of gravity between him and Jade was so intense that he surrendered to his need. He disarmed and rearmed the security system to the main house. When he entered the guest house, she was in the shower. His heart rate increased as he inhaled her orange blossom and honey body wash, all things Jade, feminine and soft. He didn't want to frighten her, but before he could whisper her name, she glanced up and saw him. He turned and walked to the bedroom.

The starlight and moonlight flowing through the window emphasized the outline of her when she entered the bedroom. He reached for her and she willingly came to him. He fitted her close in the spooning position. He kissed her hair.

Donovan whispered the name "Diamond," into her ears.

He rubbed Jade's stomach and took a deep breath before speaking, again.

"Did you want her?"

Jade spoke softly, "Yes. It didn't matter that we were still in college. It didn't matter if we were together or not. She was ours...I wanted her and you. Your internship at Sims Financial was important and I didn't want to interfere. I believed that when you returned, things would work out between us, and we would become a family. I never imagined that...I would miscarriage. My doctors said there was nothing that I could have done to prevent it."

"I could have been there with you through it all. You took that choice away from me. Jade, this pain and hurt is like nothing that I've ever experienced. I try to envision her, but I can't. I feel such a loss, but I have nothing tangible to connect this pain to but you. I am so angry with you."

"Donovan, I am sorry," Jade said.

"Yeah, me too," he responded.

"Is there anything else you want to know?" she asked.

"Will the pain ever go away?"

Jade placed her hand over Donovan's hand that still rested on her stomach.

"It lessens, but no it never leaves. I just try to remember the most important part of it all; Diamond was created by our love."

He kissed the back of her neck. "Let's go to sleep."

The next morning when Donovan woke up, Jade was gone. Next to him he found a white wooden box with an oval sterling silver emblem engraved DJJ. Inside the box were dried white rose petals, a locket, sonograms, appointment cards, a photo album, and a journal.

Donovan spent the morning looking through the contents of the box, the photo album, and reading the journal. The photo album had various pictures of him and Jade as a couple. There were journal entries actually addressed to him. From the words on the pages he'd read, Jade loved him and Diamond very much. As Donovan was about to return everything to the box, he noticed an envelope. Donovan pulled out three pictures. To his surprise, there was a copy of his and Jade's baby picture. The third picture took his breath away, his eyes filled with tears as he looked at a picture of Diamond. An artist had hand sketched a picture of a baby, with a combination of Donovan's and Jade's features. The picture of their daughter, Diamond was beautiful, perfect, and angelic. He no longer had to try to envision Diamond, her image would forever be etched in his memory. Donovan cried until he was able to release the hurt and the anger. Donovan returned everything back to the box and dialed Jade's cell number, but she didn't answer.

"Thank you."

By sharing her memory box of Diamond, Jade had given Donovan tangible things to connect his loss to. His healing journey could begin.

Chapter Twenty-Four

It had been two weeks since she'd returned home from Khalil's birthday weekend, and Jade had immersed herself in her work. Although she desired for her relationship with Donovan to survive this storm, it no longer consumed her thoughts.

Jade stood up from behind her desk, walked over to the full-length mirror, and smiled at her reflection. She had gained at least fifteen pounds in all of the right places. Jade believed that she should have cushion and curves. She looked amazing. Everyone from staff to patients had commented on it.

Her colleagues and staff had done a marvelous job in her absence. In an effort to express her gratitude, Jade bought breakfast for everyone for the past two Fridays.

She was still experiencing difficulty with the Holly Gardens project. Due to her leave of absence, several contributors and investors had pulled their funding. Jade had practically started over. The projected completion date had been moved up to September 2014, and she was disappointed.

*****

Donovan reviewed the final purchase contract of Holly Gardens and the property adjacent to it for two miles. This was his gift to Jade, his peace offering to her. Now he was free to return his focus back on a few of his other multi-million dollar land development deals; one being in Nassau, Bahamas. Gavin was working with him on this deal and they spent endless hours preparing for their meeting in the Bahamas. Both men felt guilty about the time they were spending away from their children, but the success of this deal would continue to support the life that they were accustomed to living.

"Gavin, we should only be in the Bahamas for two days, Thursday and Friday. We'll make the time up to the kids."

"Man, I'm exhausted. After we get back, I'll need at least forty-eight hours to sleep. Danielle has been amazing about helping with Sydnee."

"They do have a great relationship."

"Yes, they do. Danielle is an amazing woman!"

"You've used the words 'Danielle' and 'amazing' in your last two sentences."

"Well, it's the truth. What's up with you? You've been pretty distracted throughout this project. Are you ready for this meet--"

Donovan interrupted Gavin.

"Look, you're right. I've been distracted, irritable, and unreasonable with you and the team. Please accept my apology."

"I accept your apology. I understand the frustrations of being in love. But you need to apologize to the team and do something special for them."

"I know. I'm texting Renee, the office manager, now. She'll know what to do. We'll be ready to fly out at 4 p.m. today. Meet me at the airport."

"All right, it won't take me long to pack. I'll see you later."

*****

Donovan and Gavin's trip to the Bahamas proved to be successful. Immediately after their final meeting, their brains and bodies began to shut down. They slept the entire flight back to Atlanta. There were cars waiting for both of them at the airport.

"I've got to pick up Sydnee from Danielle," Gavin told Donovan. "Don't call me until Tuesday."

"I may not be awake by Tuesday."

They hugged and walked their separate directions.

Donovan was exhausted, but felt anxious. His need to see Jade dominated his thoughts. He decided that he would not be able to rest and have any peace if he didn't do just that. So he called Ms. Evelyn and told her about his impromptu plans.

Of course she was elated and encouraged him to go visit Jade.

He and his pilot arranged the flight out, and an hour later Donovan was on his way to Summer, GA. He wasn't sure that he'd made the right decision, and his mind raced with questions. What was Jade doing? Would she turn him away? What would she say? What would he say?

He opened the *Atlanta Journal Constitution* newspaper and his eyes landed on a quote by Maya Angelou. *"Have enough courage to trust love one more time. And always one more time."* A feeling of peace engulfed Donovan. He invaded Jade's world just as she invaded his. He didn't have a plan. He'd take it one day at a time.

Gavin called Danielle from the car to tell her that he was on his way to pick up Sydnee. When she opened the door, he smiled at the sight of her. She was beautiful. Her face was free of makeup and her hair framed her face. She was dressed in shorts and a T-shirt. Their gaze held longer than normal as he drank in the sight of her. Gavin reached for her and pulled her close. He closed his eyes as electrical currents were exchanged between them and moaned when her scent invaded his nostrils. His moan registered with his brain and his body began to respond. Gavin immediately released her and stepped back. "Hi."

"Hi, does Donovan look as tired as you?" Danielle said as she stepped aside for Gavin to enter.

"Much worse. He's gone to visit Jade."

"Oh….. okay. Was it planned? Things between them have been pretty rocky."

"I don't think so."

"Oh, well that's interesting. Have a seat and I'll go get Sydnee."

When Danielle and Sydnee entered her family room, Gavin was asleep. Danielle couldn't bring herself to wake him. She'd take him and Sydnee home in the morning. She went outside to explain to the driver that Gavin would be staying, asked him to bring Gavin's luggage in, and thanked him with a hearty tip.

She and Sydnee were able to coerce a sleepy Gavin to the downstairs guestroom and onto the bed. She removed his shoes and covered him with a blanket. Gently caressing Gavin's face, she softly kissed him on the lips. When he whispered her name, she was startled, but warmth ran through her body and landed in her heart.

"Dani, I missed you, baby."

As Danielle stared at Gavin, her heart leaped with joy. She touched her lips with the tips of her fingers. Did he feel the same way about her? Was it possible?

Danielle quietly left the room as tears formed in her eyes at the infinite possibilities.

*****

Jade was in need of some girl time. Getting together with her girls could cultivate and raise her spirits. Teresa and Monique had proven to be wonderful friends.

The three spent a day at the spa and the salon, with plans for the evening to attend the grand opening of a new supper club, *Harmony, Rhythm, and Blues*. Once they were prepared for their night, Monique and Teresa sat on the sofa waiting for Jade, who'd decided to change clothes for the third time. The doorbell rang and Monique answered the door.

"Good evening. I'm Donovan. Is Jade home?"

"Yes, hi. Please c-come in. I'm Monique, a friend of Jade's."

Teresa stood when they entered the living room; she did a head-to-toe scan of the man and smiled. It had to be Donovan. He was handsome in his tailored suit and expensive shoes. More importantly, he had luggage in his hand and a suit bag on his shoulder.

"Donovan, I'm Teresa, Jade's friend... It's a pleasure to meet you," she said, extending her hand to Donovan.

He lightly shook her hand. "The pleasure's mine."

"Jade should be down shortly. We were on our way out, but--"

Donovan's eyes looked beyond Teresa as Jade entered the room. The energy in the room shifted and everyone was aware of it.

Jade's breath caught in her throat. When she spoke his name, it came out as a whisper.

"Donovan." Jade stared at the god-like man standing in her doorway. She was at a loss for words.

"Jade."

Donovan's voice was strained. Not only did Jade look beautiful, but also she was sexy as hell in the black dress that revealed the curve of her breasts and accentuated her hips. To top it off, she was wearing the sexiest pair of shoes that he had ever seen. He fought with all of his control to prevent his body from betraying him at the first sight of her.

"Baby, you look amazing."

"Thank you. We were on our way out for a First Friday event downtown," Jade said.

Walking toward her, Donovan said, "Teresa told me. I am exhausted and jet lagged, but I couldn't go another night without seeing you. I'll probably be asleep when you get back, but enjoy yourself."

He stopped and placed his left hand on Jade's cheek. He slowly moved his mouth over her lips. He kissed her twice and licked the right corner of her mouth with the tip of his tongue.

Jade moaned with pleasure and was embarrassed when her eyes flew open. Donovan winked and smiled sensually at Jade. With that same smile, he turned to Teresa and Monique, whose mouths were open.

"It was a pleasure meeting both of you. I hope you enjoy your night."

With that, Donovan turned and walked upstairs. He smiled as he listened to the women's questions to Jade.

Jade's fragrant scent lingered in the air. Although he'd never been in Jade's home, he felt a sense of familiarity here. He opened the door to the first bedroom, certain that it was the guest room. He deposited his luggage in the closet and sat in the chair next to the window.

Jade and her friends hadn't left the house yet. He couldn't make out their conversation, but he was sure that he was the main topic.

He thought of Jade in that sexy black dress and shoes. Jealousy ran through his veins as he thought of how other men would have the privilege of seeing Jade dressed like that. Donovan took deep breaths until he felt the tension leave his body. He gathered his personal items and headed to the bathroom. He needed a long hot shower--well, maybe a cold shower.

*****

Jade placed her shawl and clutch on the back of the sofa. She walked to the kitchen with Monique and Teresa on her heels.

"Jade."

"Yes, Monique."

"Girl, um, um, um. I need more than a 'yes.' Your man is upstairs," Monique stated in her animated voice.

"I know that," Jade answered calmly.

"Did you know he was coming?" Teresa asked.

"No, I haven't talked with him in two weeks."

"What!" Monique yelled.

"Monique, not so loud. Jade, if you haven't talked to him in two weeks, why is he here?" Teresa asked.

"I don't know. Ms. Evelyn said he and Gavin were working in the Bahamas for a few days."

"I guess he finished his work in the Bahamas. From the look in his eyes and the way you were moaning, he's here to work you," Monique said.

"Monique, stop. Jade, do you want us to leave?" Teresa said with a smile.

Jade didn't answer.

"Look, Jade, there is a fine man in your house," Teresa

continued. "You don't need to go out."

"Yes, I do. Let me just fix him a snack."

"What? He doesn't need that, he needs a seven-course meal…beginning with you."

They all laughed.

Jade prepared Donovan two peanut butter, jelly, and banana sandwiches and a large glass of milk with ice. She placed the items on a tray along with bottled water, an apple, and napkins. "Look, let me take this upstairs and I'll be right back."

When she reached the door, she heard the shower running. She entered the guest bedroom and placed the tray on the side table where she was sure that he wouldn't miss it.

Jade could have easily stayed home, but she deserved to enjoy the night out with her friends. She'd deal with her and Donovan's emotional rollercoaster tomorrow. Besides, she was certain that he had come to her home to rest. Donovan was still passionate regarding his work. He had worked non-stop, around the clock in college on research projects or proposals until he arrived at her apartment to crash for two or three days. She was sure that his current stay would be the same. But inwardly she smiled; Donovan's impromptu visit assured her that he missed her as much as she missed him. He sought comfort and rest here.

Jade entered the kitchen. "Alright, ladies. I'm ready." Jade said.

"Why are you smiling? You weren't up there long enough for a quickie."

"Monique, stop that. Jade, are you sure you want to go out with us, instead of staying here with Donovan?" Teresa asked.

"Yes, let's go, ladies," Jade answered and led her friends out the house.

*****

Danielle couldn't focus on anything. She'd attempted

to read, but the romance novel's steamy sex scenes were too much and sent her celibate body into a heat wave. She plundered through the house by cleaning and reorganizing.

She had loved Gavin for a long time. Her love for him was so that she had buried her feelings in the deepest place within her. She didn't think that he'd seen her as a woman before, but only as Donovan's little sister.

She really needed to talk with someone and decided to text Jade.

"Is Donovan with you?" she texted.

"Yes, he's asleep at my house. I'm eating dinner with some friends. What's up?"

"Nothing really... Just call me when you get home."

"Okay, but it'll be late... around 12 or 1."

"LOL! That's not late."

*****

Jade had enjoyed herself. The food, music, and company at *Harmony, Rhythm, and Blues Supper Club* had been great. She'd loved the soulful songs the band had played.

She thought of Onyx and how much her sister would enjoy the good music. She could envision her sister on stage singing and playing with the band. Onyx had an amazing voice. She could evoke tears, um hums, and cheers with the melodies she created with her voice.

Jade purchased a grilled chicken salad from the Supper Club for Donovan's lunch the next day. On the way home she stopped by the grocery store to pick up lemons to make lemonade, apples, bananas, and butter pecan ice cream. All were items that Donovan used to eat during his rest and recovery period. He'd eat, shower, and go back to sleep over the course of two days. Now, after factoring in his age and the stress related to the business deal, it could very well be longer.

She arrived back home around 10:30 p.m. Donovan had left the porch light and lamp in the family room on. It hadn't surprised her to see that he'd come down to the kitchen after eating the snack. He'd washed, dried, and put the dishes away, and left her a simple note saying thank you.

Although they hadn't talked in weeks, she wanted his time in her home to be peaceful and accommodating. She'd noticed that he had lost weight. His face was much too slender and his tailored suit was no longer a perfect fit. He had reverted back to his defense mechanisms of obsessively working, preoccupying his mind, and not sleeping or eating.

Jade's eyes filled with tears; she hated being the source of his distress. She set her alarm system and walked softly up the stairs, stopping briefly at the guest room door. Surprisingly, she didn't hear Donovan's low snoring. He wasn't asleep. He'd waited for her to get home. Should she knock? No. Instead.

She decided to call Tia and Onyx.

"Onyx? Tia?"

"I'm here." Onyx answered.

"Me, too," Tia said, yawning.

"Jade, what's going on?"

"Donovan's here."

"Say again?" Onyx asked.

"I was on my way out with Monique and Teresa and he just showed up."

"What did he say?" Tia asked.

"He told me he was exhausted, he kissed me, and told me to have fun with my friends."

Yawning again, Tia inquired, "Jade, tell me you stayed home with him."

"No, I didn't and I don't regret it. I needed to get out of the house. Don't get me wrong… I'm glad that he is here."

"Jade, I say make the best of the time you have with him," Onyx said.

"I agree with Onyx. Good night," Tia said and disconnected the call.

"Onyx, he just showed up. Am I supposed to just go with

the flow?" Jade asked sarcastically.

"Yes, Jade, do you know how many women wish their men would *just show up*? Look, I've got to go. Love you. Bye."

Onyx was right. Donovan had reached out to her. She'd just accept it at face value and wait for his next move. Whatever he needed from her during his stay, she would gladly provide, especially love.

*****

Jade's phone chimed with a reminder to call Danielle back. "Hey Danielle, what's going on with you?"

"I'm good, what about you?" Danielle asked.

"I'm okay. Why?"

"Are you really okay with Donovan just showing up on your door step unannounced? He's been pretty unreasonable with you lately. I'm not sure what's going on, but you should've kicked him OUT!"

"Girl, please, it's not that easy; life's not that easy. And besides, you know that I love your brother. How did you know he was here?"

"Gavin came by to pick up Sydnee, but..."

"But what?" Jade asked.

"He's still here. He fell asleep on the couch, but with Sydnee's help, we moved him to the guest room."

"So how are you, with Gavin being so close?"

"What do you mean?"

"Danielle, you know exactly what I'm talking about."

"No, Jade, I don't."

"The fact that Donovan is sleeping in the room next to me has my heart unbalanced and my body throbbing."

"Stop! TMI," Danielle said, laughing.

"Dani, don't even pretend that Gavin asleep in your home is not affecting the woman in you."

"Please, you know Gavin and I are just friends. He's Donovan's best friend, for goodness' sake."

"You're joking, right?"

"No, I'm not. So let's change the subject."

"Fine."

Jade and Danielle chatted for about ten minutes before they said their goodbyes.

"Jade…wait! How long do you think they'll sleep?"

"I don't know, maybe a total of two to three days. Just have easy snacks, lunch tomorrow, and a hearty dinner on Sunday."

And with that last comment, Jade disconnected the call. She shook her head, wondering how long Danielle and Gavin were going to play their mating game.

*****

Jade woke to the telephone ringing. It was Monique.

"So, what happened last night?"

"What do you mean?"

"Jade, please stop. What happened between you and Donovan? Oops, is it still happening? Did I interrupt ya'll?"

"Yeah, you interrupted my sleep. Donovan is probably asleep in the guest room."

"Why aren't you sleeping next to him?"

"He's not here for that and, besides, we still have some issues to resolve. What are you doing today?"

"Nothing much, just lying around. What about you?"

"I'm coming over there to lie around with you. Let's call Teresa and make it a girl's day of doing nothing."

"Jade, you are tripping. You want to spend the day with Teresa and me? You need to talk to him."

"I know, but he is going to sleep most of the day and not feel up to talking."

"Okay, suit yourself. Come on over. Is eleven okay?"

"Perfect, we can make brunch. I'll call Cheryl."

"See you later."

*****

Donovan slept soundly until two o'clock that day.

178

Disoriented, he looked around the room, alarmed. Where was he? Then he smelled the mixture of her scent and the citrus fragrance she wore.

He spotted a note on the nightstand.

Your lunch is in the refrigerator. Enjoy and rest well.

Donovan got up and took a long, hot shower before heading downstairs to eat his lunch. He noticed the basket of assorted apples and bananas. He checked the freezer and was not disappointed. She'd bought butter pecan ice cream. The grilled chicken salad and lemonade were delicious. Jade had been thoughtful and selfless.

He felt a sharp pain of guilt for his behavior during the past couple months. He had valued thoughtful gestures. Acts of service is one of his love languages. Jade making lemonade and buying his favorite ice cream meant a lot to him. Donovan cleaned the kitchen and prepared to head upstairs to go back to sleep when he heard the phone ring. He checked the Caller ID; it was Jade's mom. Donovan debated about answering the phone and decided against it. He didn't want to explain to her why he was there.

Then he heard her voice through the answering machine: "Jade, Donovan…if you are there, pick up." He did as instructed.

"Hi, Pearl."

"Hi, sweetie. Evelyn told me you were in town. Are you and Jade coming by today?"

"I--well--"

"Donovan, well, what?" Pearl said, agitated.

"Jade's not here and I was actually about to go back to sleep."

"Where is she?"

"Her note said she was at Monique's."

"Why is she at Monique's if you're there?"

"I just returned from a business trip and have been

sleeping."

"Donovan, you could have slept at home. Why are you at Jade's if you two aren't working on your relationship?"

"It's not that easy," Donovan responded.

"Yes, it is. Look, I will not allow you to emotionally antagonize my daughter. Either you forgive her or you leave her alone until you can. Between you and this expansion deal for Holly Hill, my daughter is stressed out."

Although Pearl's tone and words were strong, Donovan heard the underlying pain. He didn't speak.

"Donovan, she loves you and you love her. When my daughter ended her relationship with you in college, she left her heart with you. She was young and made a mistake. Now it's time for you to decide if you will cherish her heart or give it back. Goodbye."

Donovan looked out the kitchen window as Pearl's words rang loudly in his ears. He had a decision to make. They'd already spent fourteen years apart.

He returned to the guest bedroom. He climbed under the covers, allowed his mind to be consumed with thoughts of loving Jade, and easily found sleep.

*****

Gavin sat up, not opening his eyes. He'd had a good nap, but he needed to get up, shower, and change into his pajamas. He wanted to check on Sydnee. He fumbled his way to the bathroom, slowly opened his eyes, and realized for the first time that he hadn't slept in his own home. His personal items were neatly arranged in the guest bath. He quickly brushed his teeth and showered. Before leaving the bathroom, Gavin stared at his reflection in the mirror. What happened? Why was he at Danielle's?

Gavin exited the guest room and walked through the entire house, only to find it empty. He was thirsty and hungry. Immediately upon entering the kitchen, he noticed the note on the dry erase board:

Hi, sleepy head. We're spending the day with Ms. Evelyn and the kids.

Your lunch is in the refrigerator.

Rest well,

Danielle

Lunch, thank goodness. He was hungry and she'd made his favorite. Chicken salad neatly placed on a bed of romaine lettuce with cherry tomatoes on the side and sweet tea to drink. Danielle was a great cook. Gavin ate and cleaned the kitchen. Then he headed to the guest room to sit down on the bed to text Danielle: "Thank you. You are amazing."

She responded immediately. "You're more than welcome."

He smiled, yawned, and was overcome by his need to sleep. He'd planned to lie down until Danielle and Sydnee returned, but once his head hit the pillow, Gavin slept for another twenty hours. When he woke again, it was three o'clock Sunday afternoon. He showered and walked down to the kitchen.

Gavin couldn't speak, as he was mesmerized by Danielle's graceful movements throughout the kitchen as she prepared dinner. Instead, he sat at the kitchen island.

"Hey, you," Danielle said over her shoulder. "Just a minute and I'll fix your coffee."

"No, I'll get it. Where's Sydnee?" Gavin asked in between yawns.

"She's upstairs studying. I already started the coffee. Creamer is in the fridge. How do you feel?"

"I am still a little tired. Do you need me to help you with anything?" He took a sip of his coffee. "Mmm, that's perfect. Good coffee."

"No, just take a seat and keep me company while I finish this up," Danielle said.

She prepared a pot roast, twice-baked potato casserole,

and green beans sautéed with red peppers, onions, and garlic. For dessert, she pulled a blueberry cobbler out of the oven, ready to be served with scoops of vanilla ice cream.

Danielle talked about work, world news, and Sydnee, who was watching television in the family room. She frequently asked him questions that he could not answer. She was beautiful, sexy, and intelligent. Although four years her senior, Gavin found himself attracted to and in love with his best friend's little sister.

He'd become aware of her for the first time on the night of her senior prom. When she'd walked down the spiral stairs towards him, her escort for the night, Gavin felt a prick in his heart and a tug in his groin. He'd immediately felt guilty for his attraction to her and buried his thoughts deep within. Now several years later, it was becoming more difficult for him to keep the feelings buried. He wasn't sure, but sometimes her eyes said that she cared for him on a different level too. Gavin worried about jeopardizing the friendship they shared.

Dinner was great and they all ate to their hearts' content. Afterward, they all decided to take a stroll around the lake. Sydnee walked between Danielle and Gavin, holding each of their hands.

*****

Jade and her friends cooked, watched romantic comedies, and relaxed. Their time together occupied her mind for the day. When Jade arrived home, Donovan was asleep. She hadn't expected him to be up, but was glad to see that he had eaten.

She planned to attend the eleven o'clock service at church the following morning. Although she was certain that Donovan would still be asleep while she attended church, she knew once he woke he'd be starving. She decided to prepare part of Sunday dinner tonight. She cooked cabbage, seasoned with smoked turkey necks and onions, cream corn, rice, and a Key Lime cake. Then she prepared the pot roast with her seasoning mixture, potatoes, onions, and carrots in her Pampered Chef deep dish baker to cook on low overnight. She decided to wait to prepare the sweet corn bread and banana pudding tomorrow. She hoped they would eat dinner and spend Sunday together.

But when Jade arrived home from church the next day, Donovan was gone. All that was left of him was his scent and another note.

Jade,

Thank you for opening your home to me and for your hospitality.
Dinner was great. I'm sorry.

Donovan

Jade's eye pooled with tears, but she refused to cry. She went to the guest room to remove the bed linens and wash them, but he'd already done that. The linens were neatly folded on the bed. Jade sat in the chair next to the bed and the tears fell over and over.

He had walked away. He said thank you, but he walked away, again.

Jade willed her heart to harden a little. She would no longer allow Donovan to control her emotions.

*****

Jade arrived at work at 6:45 a.m. to avoid anyone seeing her when she walked in. She engrossed herself in reviewing the pending contracts and proposal for the expansion of Holly Health.

At 9 a.m., she was startled by the knock on her office door. Monique entered her office, followed by someone carrying the largest, most beautiful bouquet of lilies. Jade's heart skipped.

They were from Donovan, but she refused to call him.

Bouquets of lilies in various hues arrived at Jade's office every fifteen minutes until 12:15 p.m. The last and fourteenth bouquet had a letter attached:

Jade,

We did not get a chance to speak when I was there; I just wanted to rest and be near you. Each time I close my eyes and look deep within myself, I catch a glimpse of you there. I carry you in my spirit and your heart beats inside of me. These flowers are a testament of how I feel about you, and about our relationship. I love you.

Donovan

Jade dialed Donovan's cell phone. Before he could say hello, she was talking.

"Donovan, I love you."

There was a knock on her door, but Jade didn't acknowledge it. She turned her back to the door, but it opened as she continued. "I love you, I love you, please forgive me."

"I already have. Will you forgive me? I love you, Jade Simone Michaels." The voice came from behind her.

She turned and ran to him. He picked her up and she wrapped her legs around his waist.

"I love you more, Donovan Jamal Johnson."

Monique stood in the doorway and cleared her throat.

Donovan released Jade, who slid down the length of his hard body.

Stepping away, she retrieved her purse and finally made eye contact with Monique. "Monique, I am leaving for the rest of the day."

"I would hope so. I'll cancel your appointments for tomorrow, too," Monique said in her best *you go, girl* voice.

Jade winked as she passed and said, "Thanks."

Chapter Twenty-Five

One week later. . . .

Donovan was lying across his bed reading the paper when Khalil knocked on the door and asked for permission to enter. His sisters followed and stood beside him, as if preparing for war. Although he was curious about the topic of discussion, Donovan waited for one of the children to speak first. The obvious spokesperson, Miss Kamia, stepped forward. Donovan smiled inwardly. Kamia was no longer the shy girl that she had been months before. Her verbal communication skills had improved significantly as a result of speech therapy. He was grateful for her self-confidence and inner strength. Now, she was a force to be reckon with.

"Daddy, we all love you, but we want--"She paused and looked back at her siblings for support.

"We want Jade to come home. We miss her. Will you please go get her and bring her back?"

Donovan smiled because he missed her too.

"I miss her too, but Jade has to finish a very special project. She should be home in a month."

Kamia turned the TV to *Dr. Doolittle*. Soon, one by one, the children laid across the bed to watch the movie and fall asleep. Donovan was delighted to have the kids in his space. Even Khalil lay at the bottom of the bed.

Donovan smiled at the children. It was the complete sense of family that made this experience wonderful.

His thoughts were interrupted by his cell phone ringing. It was Jade. Donovan's feeling of delight soon turned into concern. Jade was not a night owl and usually didn't call after 10 p.m.

"Hello, sweetheart. I was just thinking about you. Why are

you up so late?"

Jade couldn't find her voice.

Donovan instinctively knew that something was wrong. Jade began sobbing.

"Jade, please tell me what's going on."

Jade explained that she had a meeting with everyone involved with the Holly Gardens project that coming Thursday.

"I am not sure if I have any fight left in me. This project is in memory of Jonothan."

"Yes, you do. The Jade I know and love would never give up a fight," he smiled. Unbeknownst to Jade, the victory was already hers. "Would you like for me to come to the meeting with you?"

"No, this is something I need to take care of alone, but thank you for offering. You are right; they better be ready for me."

"That's right, babe, they better. Now since you seem better about your meeting, let me tell you what our kids did today."

She had heard right. He said "our kids" loud and clear. She giggled because there was no telling what their kids had done. Settling deep into her covers, she laughed at all the details Donovan provided. He had learned to imitate all of the kids perfectly.

She was ready to go home. She missed her man and her kids.

*****

Donovan heard Kamill's voice. "Daddy, Daddy!"

All the hairs on his body stood up. "Oh God," he whispered to himself. Donovan leapt out of the chair he'd been lying in, since the children had taken over the bed. The other children were already awake.

"What is it, sweetie?" He feared what she'd dreamed about this time. Kamill's gift of dreams was a blessing, one that evoked a range of emotions.

Kamill smiled through her tears. "Jade is coming home."

Donovan inhaled deeply as a feeling of serenity washed over him. He smiled back and said, "Yes, baby, she is coming home," as he scanned the faces of his children. They were all smiles.

Chapter Twenty-Six

Donovan planned to politely interrupt Jade's meeting with the City Council, though his flight left later than scheduled.

The City Hall building was old and small. Donovan hurried down the stuffy and musky hallway to the meeting room. He entered the room in a rush and spotted Jade. She looked totally defeated and it broke his heart. He went to her, pulled her into his arms, and kissed her on the forehead.

"Jade, baby, everything will be all right."

"No, Donovan, it won't be. Someone else purchased Holly Gardens and the land adjacent to it."

"Everything will be fine." He released her and walked toward the members of the City Council. He cleared his throat to be acknowledged. "Good afternoon, gentlemen."

"Good afternoon, Mr. Johnson. You're early," the City Council President stated. "If you would wait in the lobby, we will meet with you shortly."

"Good afternoon. It was my intent to arrive and participate in this meeting with Ms. McNeir. However, my flight was delayed. It is with great pleasure that I inform you that I purchased Holly Gardens to make someone very special to me dreams come true."

"How nice, but again, we need to conclude this meeting, Mr. Johnson."

"Well, let me save you the trouble. Ms. McNeir is that special someone," Donovan said, walking toward Jade.

"Donovan?"

"Here, sweetheart, these are for you," he said as he placed the land deeds in Jade's hand.

Jade was overjoyed. Donovan had made her vision for Holly Gardens a reality. He had purchased Holly Gardens, the land adjacent to it, and other prime real estate in the city in the name of J. Simone Michaels, her maiden name.

Donovan resumed the meeting and quickly established the

expectations for the project. He presented the state, city, and all parties with modified contracts and permits. Jade smiled. She was just as surprised as the members of the City Council were upon discovering that Jade McNeir and J. Simone Michaels were one and the same.

Later that evening, after the meeting with the City Council, Jade and Donovan met with Jonothan's parents at their home. Jade introduced them to Donovan. She explained her plans of returning to Atlanta to live, but returning periodically to Summer to continue working with Holly Health and overseeing the Holly Gardens renovation project.

"Jade, we wish you all the happiness your heart can hold," Mrs. McNeir said as they walked Jade and Donovan to the door.

"She is a jewel, son, love her like such," Mr. McNeir said as he shook Donovan's hand.

"I already do, sir."

Mr. McNeir released Donovan's hand, "Good, because me and a few friends would hate to have to pay you a visit."

"Honey, behave." Mrs. McNeir said. "Both of you, please stop by and visit when you're in town."

Donovan reached for Jade's hand and responded. "We will."

Once in the car, Jade spoke first, "that was easier than I thought."

"I'm glad. They seem to genuinely care about you."

"They do, but Tia and her parents have been my life line to Jonothan. I never really expected their blessings or approval," Jade admitted.

"Well, it worked out. Are you okay?" Donovan asked.

"Yes, I'm more than okay."

Jade and Donovan tied up loose ends on Friday. By Saturday afternoon, they were aboard Donovan's plane heading back to Atlanta. Jade was able to breathe for the first time in months. With no more secrets or remnants from the past, she could freely love Donovan.

Chapter Twenty-Seven

Later Saturday evening…

Jade was inundated with anticipation. She hadn't seen the children in two months. When they arrived at the house, Jade expected to be greeted at the door, but no one was there. The house was unusually quiet.

Then Jade heard music echoing from the garden. When she opened the French doors that led outside, she was pleasantly surprised.

The garden was beautifully decorated with flowers, ribbon, and candles in cream and various shades of pink and green with accents of silver. Tears pooled in Jade's eyes and she looked to Donovan, who gestured toward the path of roses. Jade carefully followed the lined path of rose petals until she saw the children, his family, and their friends. She recognized the song that echoed throughout the garden: "Made to Love You" by Gerald Levert.

The children greeted her with hugs and kisses. Donovan smiled with happiness as he witnessed the emotional exchange between Jade and the children.

When the children released Jade, they stepped to the side, and Donovan walked towards her. He reached for her left hand and went down on one knee. "Jade Simone, you complete me. I want to love you and cherish you forever. Will you marry me?"

Donovan felt Jade's body tremble. He placed his hands around her waist to secure her.

"Yes!"

Donovan placed a 2.38 ct. pink oval-shaped diamond ring set in rose gold on Jade's finger, stood up, and kissed her.

When Jade opened her eyes, she saw Tia and the girls standing next to her. Khalil and a minister were next to

Donovan.

"What's going on?" she whispered.

"Will you marry me today? Right now?"

Jade looked between Donovan, the children, his parents, Danielle, Gavin, Sydnee, and Amelia; then to her friends Tia, Emanuel, Teresa, and Monique; everything was perfect, except that she didn't see her mom, Onyx, or her family.

Then an angelic soulful voice began to sing "Sweet Love" by Anita Baker. For a moment Jade thought the song was playing only in her head, but then she saw her mother and sister walking towards her. Her mother's eyes focused on Jade, but Onyx's eyes were focused in another direction. Jade glanced in the direction that held her sister's gaze hostage and saw a ruggedly handsome man who looked vaguely familiar.

Joshua, a member of the United States Army Elite Special Forces, was most vulnerable at this moment. The air in his lungs stood still when he heard her voice; then he saw her. She was breathtakingly beautiful. Joshua blinked several times and initiated air flow back to his lungs. God had a sense of humor beyond anything he could fathom. Then her name escaped his lips: "Onyx." It was at that exact moment her eyes found him and it felt like only she was sharing this moment and space in time with him. When they reached Jade, her mom stepped forward to embrace her. Pearl whispered, "Your father is smiling down from heaven. We're all here to give you our love and support on your wedding day."

Jade looked around again and saw her family and Jonothan's parents. The people that she loved the most had suddenly appeared and now everything was perfect.

She turned to Donovan and said: "Yes, I will marry you today." She kissed him long and hard.

Everyone applauded.

When Jade ended the kiss, Tia stepped up and said, "Okay, that's enough. Please excuse us."

Onyx and Tia led Jade into the house.

"Who helped Donovan plan this?" Jade asked, looking

between Tia and Onyx. "And who is the guy that you were singing to, Onyx?"

"I asked her the same thing," Tia chimed in.

Onyx took a deep breath and smiled at her sister, all the while her insides quivered from its reaction to the man whom she had indeed found herself singing to.

"It's Joshua, my Joshua," Onyx signed.

"OMG, Joshua, the guy!" Tia yelled.

"Oh, the guy who has you strung out!" Jade said.

"Yep," Onyx said and found a place to sit down.

It was really him. She closed her eyes and took a deep breath in hopes to calm herself. With her eyes closed, her mind replayed visions of a space in time...

"I can't believe this, you are getting hot and bothered over there! Get up Onyx and help me get dressed."

"Onyx!"

In twenty minutes, Jade was dressed in a beautiful fitted ivory dress that flared at the ankles, and a five-foot train, a veil, something old, and something new--you name it; she had it.

"Onyx and Tia, thank you. You brought Donovan back into my life and now this wedding, this dress...I know that you helped Donovan plan this for me," Jade said, tearing up.

"Jade, please don't cry; your makeup," Tia responded. "Stop that." She persisted.

"Jade, we love you so much and you deserve the joy that Donovan brings to your life. Now *come on*, let's get you married," Onyx said, gently squeezing Jade's hands.

Donovan stood under the garden's gazebo dressed in an ivory tuxedo. Natalie was her bridesmaid, Kamia and Kamill were flower girls, and Khalil was the best man. Everything was perfect.

Jade walked down the pink rose petal-covered aisle to Eric Bennett and Tamia's "Spend My Life with You."

Donovan and Jade were married surrounded by their friends and family. The ceremony and the reception were a true reflection of their love for one another and the importance of family.

Joshua continued to linger in the background, not wanting to disrupt this special day for Donovan. Then he felt a hand on his shoulder.

"Welcome home."

"Thanks, man. I was away on a mission that couldn't be interrupted, even for the notification of my brother's death. I just got back to the states ten days ago and was told to contact you. I tried to call you today, but didn't get a response, so I just dropped by. I'm glad that I did. Congratulations," Joshua responded as they embraced each other.

Both men held each other and fought back tears. They found comfort as they released their emotions into one another.

Jade noticed Donovan speaking to a man near the edge of the garden. Then she was overwhelmed with a strange feeling and became aware of the man's identity. He shared the same face as Khalil and Natalie. Onyx's Joshua and Nathan's twin brother Joshua were one in the same. Jade approached the men quietly, but as usual, Donovan sensed her presence and turned toward her.

"Jade, this is Joshua, Nathan's twin brother."

Joshua extended his hand, but Jade embraced him. "Welcome to our home. I'm so glad that you're here. "

"Thank you for having me. Now I don't feel like I crashed your wedding. I've been in town for a few days working through all of this. I tried to call you, but I couldn't reach you. I needed to see the kids and couldn't stay away any longer."

"No, please don't apologize," Jade said.

"Have you seen Natalie and Khalil?" Donovan asked.

"I've watched them from here. I didn't want to disrupt the occasion."

"Sweetheart, please excuse us. There is something that I need to give Joshua. After we're done, he can speak with the kids." Donovan kissed her gently before leading Joshua to the main house.

Donovan and Joshua entered into the house and Donovan led Joshua to his office. He retrieved an envelope from the safe and gave it to Joshua.

"Nathan left this letter for you."

"A letter," Joshua laughed before speaking, "He was always a writer. He believed letters and notes were more personal than emails or texts. Thank you."

"How long will you be in town?"

"At least two months."

"Good, Jade and I are only going away for two days. So we'll have plenty of time to talk when we get back. I'll give you some privacy. Take all the time you need. Feel free to re-join us outside when you're done."

"Thank you."

Joshua heard a soft knock on the door. He wiped his face; reading the letter was bittersweet.

"Uncle Josh, it's me," Natalie said softly.

Joshua wiped his face again and opened the door.

Natalie embraced Joshua, who held her in an equally strong embrace. Tears flowed down her face. "Shhhhh, Butterfly," Joshua said, referring to Natalie by her nickname. "This is a happy day. And I believe your dad is here witnessing this day of love." Then he lifted her face to his. "I'm sorry I wasn't here before, but I'm here now."

"How long will you be here?" Khalil asked, finally stepping into view.

"At least two months. So we have plenty of time."

"I'm glad you're here," Khalil said.

"So am I," he said, embracing his nephew.

"Go clean your faces and meet me in the kitchen; we need to get back to the party."

When Joshua left the office, he found Onyx standing in the kitchen looking out the bay window.

Onyx had come in to check on the older family members and guests who were sitting inside the house. As she stood there, she felt a strange sensation. Then she felt his hand on the small of her back, causing a hot surge throughout her body. She turned and their faces were inches apart.

"Joshua."

"Onyx, you look beautiful."

"Thank you. What are you doing...?"

She was interrupted by the sudden appearance of Natalie and Khalil.

Onyx smiled nervously.

Joshua stepped back from Onyx. "Excuse us, Onyx. All right, kids, let's go dance."

Joshua felt someone staring at him. He searched the crowd to find Onyx's mother. She looked at him as if he was a puzzle for which she had yet to find the missing pieces.

"Pearl, what has your mind so preoccupied that you are missing out on these precious moments?" Ms. Evelyn asked.

Pearl spoke softly, "Jade and Donovan are so happy."

"Yes, they are." Ms. Evelyn's gaze found them dancing together.

"My prayer is for Onyx to find her soul mate. She is so much like me. I wasn't sold on love and the happy ever after, until I met their father," Pearl said.

Ms. Evelyn smiled. "I don't think you have to worry about Onyx. Have you noticed the sparks that are flying between her and Joshua?"

"Yes, but I've never known my daughter to react to a man in such a way."

When there was an announcement for the bouquet toss, Pearl ushered Onyx to the middle of the floor and said, "Good luck." Onyx didn't know whether to be embarrassed or angry, but there were several other women gathered in the same space, with the hope that love would find them soon.

Jade noticed that Onyx's eyes were full of fire. Amelia and Danielle both remained seated with looks of dismay on their faces. Love was in the air and those three were in need of it.

Jade teased the women who were gathered by, pretending to toss the bouquet twice. Then she moved in to whisper something to them. She and the group of other women made a path through the guests that led straight to Danielle. Jade leaned down and whispered something in Danielle's ear, "I was told that this was for you."

Danielle was shocked by Jade's words, "What?" Jade handed Danielle the bouquet as everyone "Oohed" and "Awwed."

"I Gotta Be" by Jagged Edge echoed through the garden as Gavin made his way down the path to Danielle. He reached for her hand and she stood with him. He kissed her softly on the lips and whispered words in her ear that created a contagious smile on her face. They made their way to the center of the dance floor. Gavin gently pulled her close, as Danielle rested her head on his chest. Everyone clapped as Gavin and Danielle openly acknowledged, for the first time, the love they'd stored in their hearts for years.

Joshua walked towards Onyx. His strong eyes held her gaze and her body anticipated interaction with him, knowing the magnitude of his touch. Onyx looked away from his intense gaze. Her mind yelled, "Walk away! Walk away!" But she couldn't move. Onyx's mind surrendered to the words her heart yelled, "It's him. Don't move!" Everything still felt like a dream to Onyx. In a few moments he would be touching her, holding her. She unconsciously whispered his name. "Joshua." Joshua had changed her perception of love, he had branded her…knowingly or unknowingly…she couldn't stop herself from wanting him.

"May I have this dance?"

"Yes, I'd love to dance." When her eyes found him, the world stood still and it felt like she was sharing the moment only with him. She went into his embrace and whispered, "I've missed you."

The distraction created an opportunity for Donovan and Jade to discretely leave their reception.

"Come on." Donovan ushered Jade to the left side of the garden, to a section that she had never seen.

The path was defined by diamond-shaped flat stones surrounded by the greenest grass. A pergola covered with jasmine and ivy veins provided shade to the area. Lavender-colored lanterns hung strategically from the pergola. To the right, a white wicker love seat with lavender cushions sat in front of a man-made pond that glistened as if specks of diamonds were sprinkled in the water.

The path widened and led to another sitting area, decorated with white wicker furniture covered in lavender, pink, and sage seat cushions. A sage throw monogrammed with the pink letters DJ was draped across the white wicker rocking chair. Jade saw the statue of a little girl with angel wings releasing a butterfly. On a large stone that rested at the feet of the angel, the inscription read, "Angels gather here in Diamond's Corner."

Emotions beyond anything Jade had ever experienced flooded her senses. Donovan had created a magical place in memory of their daughter, a daughter whom he was still grieving for.

"In the spring, lilies and roses will bloom. You were wearing the color lavender the first time I saw you in college and you were wearing lavender the second time I found you. I hope that we can share this space and heal together," he said, gently wiping her tears.

Donovan led Jade around the corner to another section of the garden. It too had lavender-colored lanterns hanging from a tree with a white wicker rocking chair and a small side table nestled under the tree. He and Jade walked hand in hand to the pond with lily pads floating on the water. On the right side of the pond was a statue of a little girl with angel wings kneeling, holding a puppy. A large stone read, "May peace and grace dwell here in Amber's Place."

Jade didn't realize that she wasn't breathing until Donovan touched her arm. Too overwhelmed with emotions, Jade breathlessly whispered, "Thank you. Thank you. I love you."

"I love you more," he whispered. Donovan led Jade

through the side gate of the garden. "Sweetheart, we have to leave now. There is a car waiting for us."

"Wait! We have to tell the children goodbye," Jade said.

"Babe, they'll be out in a few minutes," Donovan said, ushering her into the limo. When they both were seated comfortably, he placed gentle kisses on her forehead and nose before capturing her mouth.

Jade broke the kiss and said, "Donovan. I just got back. It's too soon for me to leave them."

"I thought that you would say that, so I arranged something for this weekend only. It's simple, but it will be our time together," he said.

"Where are we going?" she asked.

"I reserved us the honeymoon suite at the Chateau Elan Winery and Resort located in Braselton, Georgia."

"Thank you. I promise we can go somewhere for a week or more later."

"Jade, later is the first two weeks in December and that is non-negotiable. I want to take my wife on a real honeymoon."

"Okay, but maybe the first two weeks of Jan--"

Jade stopped speaking mid-sentence when she heard Kamia's confident voice yell, "Mommy, please open the door. Let me in!"

Tears pooled in Jade's eyes. She never thought that she'd hear a child call her mommy. It sounded like music; then she heard a chorus of music:

"Mom, Dad, open the door!" Kamill yelled.

Donovan laughed, "Those are your loud children."

"Yes, they are...please open the door," she responded with a smile.

Donovan smiled at the delight in Jade's eyes. He opened the door and the kids flooded into the limo. It took fifteen minutes of hugs, kisses, and promises before they left for their "two-day" honeymoon.

Jade snuggled close to Donovan in the limo and instantly drifted into a deep sleep. Donovan looked into the face of his wife and the mother of his children. She looked angelic. He laughed and was tempted to kiss her, but he decided to let her rest for their first night together as man and wife.

When Jade woke, she and Donovan were lying in the middle of a luxurious bed. The room was illuminated with candlelight from at least one hundred cinnamon, sandalwood, and vanilla scented candles.

"Hi, beautiful. I thought you would sleep the night away. I'll order us a late dinner."

"I'm not hungry for food. I want to make love to my husband. So let's skip dinner, share a quick shower, and make love until I can't feel my legs."

"Ummm, that's sounds--"

Jade captured his words with her mouth. She moaned at the anticipation of his touch, his kiss, and their lovemaking.

The removal of their clothes and their shower were sensual foreplay for Jade and Donovan. He carried Jade to the bed, kissed her all over, and then joined their bodies. Moving slowly and deeply, he reacquainted himself with her body as it opened to take every inch of him. He moaned sweetly when he buried himself to the hilt. Whispering sensual, soul-stirring pleasure messages to him, she clinched her pelvis muscles, wrapped her legs around Donovan's, and rested her feet on the back of his knees to hold him captive until their breathing was no longer erratic.

"I love you with all that I am," Jade said, as tears of joy and love made a river down the sides of her face.

"I love you with all that I am," Donovan replied, kissing her tears and resuming their lovemaking. He was where he belonged, and she belonged to him, heart and soul.

Epilogue

Thanksgiving Day

J ade opened her eyes and was startled to find Natalie looking at her with a smile.

"Good morning, Mom. Happy Thanksgiving," Natalie whispered and kissed Jade on the cheek.

Jade was flooded with emotions. This was Natalie's first time calling her mom.

"Good morning, Butterfly. Happy Thanksgiving. Why are you awake already?" Jade whispered.

"Nana Pearl, Granny, and I are going to start cooking Thanksgiving breakfast and dinner. We agreed to start cooking at five this morning. I wanted to get up earlier than that to make coffee and have bagels ready for them."

"Oh, that's very thoughtful. I'll get up with you."

"No, Mom, you rest. I'm okay."

"Are you sure?"

"Yes, ma'am," Natalie answered.

"Okay. I love you."

"I love you more," Natalie said as she slid out of the bed.

"I love you the most," Jade said.

Jade attempted to keep her tears at bay, but couldn't. God had smiled on her. He had restored her life and filled it to the brim with love.

Jade smiled at the sight of the twins huddled together in their bed. She knew that Donovan's inner clock would wake him soon. It was going to be priceless to see his face when he found the twins in their bed, again.

Then like clockwork, Donovan's eyes popped open at 4:30 a.m. He wasn't surprised to find Jade spooning him, her bottom pressed into his groin. Then he became aware of the hand on his face. Kamill was lying behind him and Kamia was lying in front of Jade. He kissed Jade and nibbled on the back of her neck.

Jade stirred. "Hi."

"Hi. Are you okay?"

"Yes, are you?"

"No, I need to put my foot down to get these girls out of our bed or we need a bigger bed," he yawned. He had spoken with the twins numerous times about sleeping in their room all night.

"I'll order a bigger bed tomorrow. Your foot isn't working. Now, go back to sleep." Jade snuggled closer and whispered, "Happy Thanksgiving and I love you."

"Happy Thanksgiving, sweetheart. I love you more."

Donovan was thankful for the gift of loving Jade beyond the chambers of his heart.

About the Author

LaShayla Teemer Dyer was born and raised in Albany, Georgia and is a proud graduate of Dougherty Comprehensive High School. She earned both a Bachelor of Arts in Sociology and a Master of Social Work from Valdosta State University. She is a Licensed Clinical Social Worker, and she is passionate about helping people. Her social work philosophy is, "In order to help people, we have to meet them where they are.

LaShayla married her best friend from college, Kendrick. They live in Valdosta, Georgia with their two wonderful sons.

Visit her at www.lashaylateemerdyer.com